Real Kids Real Adventures™

NUMBER

DEBORAH MORRIS

Deborah Morris

B
BERKLEY BOOKS, NEW YORK

This book was previously published by Broadman & Holman Publishers as *Real Kids, Real Adventures #4*.
REAL KIDS, REAL ADVENTURES #1: A SUDDEN SHARK ATTACK!

A Berkley Book / published by arrangement with the author

PRINTING HISTORY
Broadman & Holman Publishers edition published 1995
Berkley edition published August 1997

The Putnam Berkley World Wide Web site address is
http://www.berkley.com

ISBN: 0-425-15938-8

Library of Congress Cataloging-in-Publication Data

Morris, Deborah, 1956-
    Real kids real adventures / Deborah Morris. — Berkley ed.
        p.   cm.
    Originally published: Nashville, Tenn. : Broadman & Holman
Publishers, c1994-<c1995   >.
    Contents: 2. Over the edge ; Kidnapped! ; Swept underground —
3. Tornado! ; Hero on the Blanco River ; Bear attack!
    ISBN 0-425-15975-2 (pbk. : v.2). — ISBN 0-425-16043-2 (pbk. : v. 3)
    1. Christian biography—United States—Juvenile literature.
2. Children—United States—Biography—Juvenile literature.
[1. Survival.   2. Adventure and adventurers.   3. Christian
biography.]   I. Title.
[BR1714.M67   1997]
277.3'082'0922—dc21
[B]   97-5391
                                                              CIP
                                                              AC

BERKLEY®
Berkley Books are published by The Berkley Publishing Group,
200 Madison Avenue, New York, New York 10016,
a member of Penguin Putnam Inc.
BERKLEY and the "B" design
are trademarks belonging to Berkley Publishing Corporation.

PRINTED IN THE UNITED STATES OF AMERICA

10   9   8   7   6   5   4   3   2   1

Wet ·N· Wild

A hard, foamy wave started toward Melissa. She tensed, waiting for just the right moment to jump. The trick was to let the water smoothly sweep you up off your feet instead of crashing into you. She liked trying to time it just right.

Closer . . . closer . . . *now*!

With a happy squeal, she kicked off from the sandy ocean bottom. But at that very instant, something razor sharp clamped down on her right leg, holding her down. The wave slammed into her, filling her mouth and nose with salty water. She was still sputtering when something jerked her all the way under the murky green water.

The first shock left her frozen, unable to move or even think . . . With a water-choked scream, she clawed at the sand with both hands and then doubled her left leg under her. She pushed up from the bottom with a mighty heave. But something still had hold of her right leg, pinning her down . . .

A huge shark had her right leg clamped in its jaws!

DON'T MISS OTHERS IN THE SERIES!

Real Kids Real Adventures™ #2

Coming in September 1997

Real Kids Real Adventures™ #3

Coming in October 1997

To my 102-year-old grandmother
Beatrice Hyacinth Snyder,
who showed me the magic of books.

Real Kids
Real Adventures™

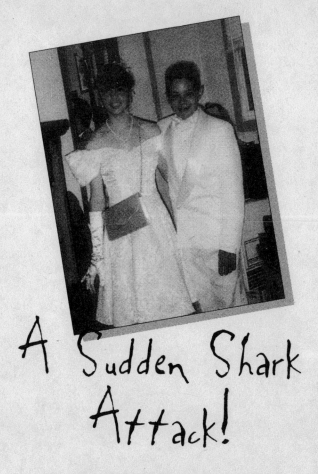

A Sudden Shark Attack!

THE MELISSA RODRIQUEZ STORY

ABOVE: Melissa Rodriquez and her cousin Tyree.

Melissa held her breath, trying not to rustle her long white dress. Beside her, her cousin, Tyree, fidgeted and tugged at his bow tie. Melissa finally poked him.

"Stop it, *Papito!*" she hissed, clutching her basket of flower petals. "It's almost time!"

Tyree, thirteen, had been stuck with the Spanish nickname "Papito" when he was a baby. Now he rolled his eyes. Melissa was four months younger than him, but she always insisted that girls were *much* more mature. He had learned a long time ago that it didn't do any good to argue with her.

Melissa tossed her dark hair impatiently and peeked around the doorway. Her aunt's wedding should start any second.

It was hard to tell, looking around, that they were on a boat. Aunt Delia had rented a small yacht for the day, and the wedding was being held down inside the cabin. The reception afterward would be up on the deck.

When the music started, Melissa stiffened. "Let's go!" she whispered. "And remember not to walk too fast."

Linking arms with Tyree, she started into the room, pausing after each step like she had practiced. Cameras flashed everywhere, and all the guests turned around in their seats to smile at them. Melissa pasted a big grin on her face and scattered a handful of flower petals on the floor, hoping she didn't look as dumb as she felt. Being a flower girl was kind of embarrassing.

It was too bad, she thought, that her mother hadn't been able to come. Her asthma had been really bad lately, and she had been afraid to leave their home in Brooklyn, New York. Melissa was the only one from her family to be there.

Joey Reyes, Melissa's uncle-to-be, was already waiting at the front. As she approached, he caught her eye and winked. She laughed. Joey had been dating Aunt Delia for over three years, and Melissa liked him a lot. He was handsome and funny, perfect for her fun-loving young aunt.

One by one, the bridesmaids marched down the aisle and took their places at the front. Then the "Wedding March" started playing, and everybody stood up to watch the bride come in.

Melissa gasped when she saw her aunt. Delia Rodriquez wore a long, white gown covered with lace and little white pearls, with a ring of white flowers in her dark hair. Melissa hoped that someday, when it was time for her to get married, she could talk her aunt into giving her the dress.

The ceremony only took a few minutes. As soon

as it was over, everybody crowded into the next room where a big, fancy dinner was waiting.

"When you finish eating," Aunt Delia announced, "go on up to the deck. We've got a band waiting up there, and we're going to have games and prizes for all the kids. It'll be party time!"

Melissa and Tyree wolfed down some chicken and roast beef, then charged up the stairs. In the late afternoon sun, the sky was a clear blue, the water peaceful. Thank goodness it hadn't decided to storm today!

Soon Aunt Delia and Uncle Joey stepped out on the deck, surrounded by a laughing crowd. The band started playing "A Whole New World" from Disney's *Aladdin* movie.

Uncle Joey grinned and put his arm around Delia. "We get the first dance!" he said, pulling her out into the middle of the deck. "Come on, *Mrs.* Reyes!"

Melissa and Tyree giggled as the newlyweds waltzed happily around the deck. But the minute the music stopped, Aunt Delia waved for everybody else to join them.

"Everybody get out here!" she shouted. "Now we're going to do the hokey-pokey!"

Melissa's mouth dropped open. She looked over at her cousin. "The hokey-pokey? She's got to be kidding! In her *wedding dress*?"

But Tyree was already moving forward. "Now *this* is what I call a wedding! Come on. Don't be a wimp."

Melissa hesitated, then followed him. Her aunt was one crazy lady!

"OK!" Aunt Delia said when everybody had crowded into a big circle. "Now we all have to sing. Here we go! You put your right arm in, you put your right arm out. You put your right arm in, and you shake it all about."

Melissa sang along, almost tripping when she got to the part about turning yourself around. Across the deck, her aunt and uncle were laughing so hard they could barely sing. Leave it to Aunt Delia to think up a wild wedding!

After the hokey-pokey they all did the "YMCA" song, forming the letters with their arms. Then a big group decided to do the Electric Slide.

Melissa didn't know the steps, so she backed away to watch. Tyree didn't know how to do it either, but he ran over to line up with the others as the band started into the twangy country tune.

At first he followed along as everybody around him began to step, slide, kick, step, slide. Soon, however, he was hopelessly out of step. Melissa giggled as he ran into people on both sides of him.

"Way to go, Papito!" she shouted. "Knock everybody down!"

At the front of the group another cousin, Ismael, was dancing smoothly. When the song ended, Aunt Delia declared him the Electric Slide winner. She handed him his prize: a small plastic guitar. Ismael, grinning, strummed it and started singing off-key to torture everybody.

The sun dipped lower in the sky. As the sky grew dark, the yacht's lights slowly twinkled on, reflecting in the water as they cruised along. Aunt Delia suggested a game of charades, and Melissa joined in. Her little cousin Stacy ended up winning the prize, a jeweled hair pin.

The stars came out. The celebration went on. It was almost midnight before Aunt Delia and Uncle Joey decided it was time to leave. The yacht docked to let everybody off.

Melissa ran over to hug her aunt. "This was a lot of fun, *Titi*," she said. In Spanish, "aunt" is *tia*. Melissa had called Delia "Titi" ever since she was a little girl.

"I'm glad," her aunt said. "Thanks for being such a pretty flower girl. And just think, in a couple of days we'll be leaving for our big trip to Florida. We're going to have so much fun!"

"I can't wait," Melissa said. "I've never been on a honeymoon before."

Her aunt laughed. "Me either. I guess it'll be a little different, bringing the whole family along, but it'll be fun. Joey and I would probably get lonely if we just went by ourselves."

"Yeah, I bet." Melissa shook her head. "You guys are nuts."

Aunt Delia and Uncle Joey had decided months before to make their wedding and honeymoon a family event. Most of the family—four adults and six kids—would be driving to Florida together to see Disney World and Wet 'n' Wild. Melissa was looking forward to it.

OFF TO DISNEY WORLD

A few days later, it was time to go. Melissa packed all her hot-weather clothes, including her favorite hot-pink bathing suit with black-and-white checked suspenders. She arrived at Aunt Delia's house, suitcase in hand, and climbed into the rented minivan with Tyree and Stacy.

Aunt Haydee and Uncle Willy were going to follow in their own van with Ismael, Giovanni, and six-year-old Willy Jr., called Wiwie for short. They planned to spend the Fourth of July together at Disney World. It would be great!

Once they were on the road, Tyree turned to Melissa. "So, are you going to learn to swim while we're in Florida? Or are you going to just sit around on the beach like a turtle?"

"I'm scared of deep water," Melissa said. "I'll probably just stay in the shallow part with Stacy and Wiwie."

"You're scared of *everything*!" Tyree retorted. "Bugs, frogs, snakes . . ." He opened his eyes wide and pointed down to her leg. "Ewwww! A big fat spider is crawling right up your leg!"

Melissa gave him a that's-not-funny look, but still glanced down to make sure there was nothing there. Tyree howled with laughter. "See? You need to get over being scared about stuff. I can teach you how to swim while we're at the beach."

"I don't want to. I'd rather hang out with Stacy." Melissa put her arm around her seven-year-old cousin. "*She* doesn't tease me about bugs. Right, Stacy?"

The little girl gave her a dimpled smile. "Right."

Aunt Delia had brought along a lot of games and books. She warned the kids that it would take two days to drive all the way down to Orlando, Florida.

"Don't even bother asking if we're there yet," she told them. "I'll tell you when we get there. If you nag me too much, I might just put you out on the side of the road and make you walk."

Melissa spent the first day in the van playing with the Game Boy, talking to Tyree and Stacy, and taking naps. It was pretty boring until Uncle Willy got stopped by a policeman for speeding. All the kids in Aunt Delia's van laughed and pointed when Uncle Willy pulled over. Aunt Delia stopped, too. They all watched as the policeman wrote out the ticket.

"Oooh, Uncle Willy looks upset," Melissa said. "Aunt Haydee doesn't look too happy either."

"You guys better quit laughing," Uncle Joey said, trying to hide his own smile. "Willy might decide to drown you when he gets you out at the beach."

"He can't swim, so he couldn't catch me," Tyree said. "I'd just swim out to where the water's over his head."

"Don't be so sure . . . he might still find a way. You better watch your step," laughed Uncle Joey.

They drove until they got tired, then pulled into a motel to get a few hours' sleep. They wanted to get to Orlando early the next day so they could go straight to Disney World.

Waking up the next morning wasn't hard for the kids. They had all slept a lot in the van. But the adults were all groaning. They staggered outside, rubbing their eyes.

"Maybe we should just sleep in and go to Disney World tomorrow," Aunt Haydee said as she carried her bag out to the van. "I'd like to be awake when I see it."

"No, Mama!" Wiwie protested. "We want to go there today! If we go tomorrow we'll miss the fireworks!"

Even Aunt Delia looked tired. "We're going; we're going," she sighed. "Just don't be so loud, OK? It makes my head hurt."

Melissa and Tyree exchanged a smile. Aunt Delia and Uncle Joey probably wished now that they'd taken a normal honeymoon without kids!

In Orlando they quickly checked into their hotel, then headed to Disney World. The kids were all jumping up and down with excitement by the time they drove through the front entrance.

"Look!" Melissa said, pointing out the window. "All those big bushes are trimmed to look like Mickey Mouses!"

"Mickey Mice," corrected Tyree. "Or maybe it's Mickey Meese."

Aunt Delia laughed. "One's a *Minnie* Mouse. And see how the flowers have been planted to make a Mickey face?"

"It's pretty," said Stacy softly. "I like it."

After parking both vans, they all got out and stood in line. It looked like about a million other people had decided to go to Disney World for the

Fourth of July. Aunt Haydee had brought her video camera along so she could film their whole day.

When they finally got inside, Melissa looked around in awe. Cinderella's Castle towered up above the trees far across the park. Everywhere she looked there were rides, or balloons, or cartoon figures walking around hugging people. Music and laughter filled the air. When a big Goofy walked past, waving, Stacy hid behind Melissa. She wasn't crazy about big furry dog-people who tried to grab her.

"Let's go!" Tyree said impatiently. "I want to go on Space Mountain first!"

From that moment on, the kids raced wildly from one ride to the next, dragging the four adults along. After they went on Space Mountain, It's a Small World and the Snow White ride, Tyree and Giovanni started teasing Melissa for only wanting to go on the "baby" rides.

"How could you get scared on the Snow White ride?" Giovanni demanded in disbelief. "Stacy and Wiwie weren't even scared. Even a tiny *baby* wouldn't be scared! You're the only human being in the entire *world* who'd be scared of that!"

"I wasn't scared," Melissa protested. "I just didn't like it, that was all. I liked the Small World ride better. I want to go on that one again."

"I don't want to see a bunch of stupid dolls singing, 'It's a small world' a hundred more times," Tyree said. "Why don't we go back to Space Mountain?"

"No way," said Melissa. "I liked watching the

shooting stars and stuff while we were in line, but I hated the part where it went pitch black and you started falling."

"That was the best part," Tyree said. "Girls are such babies."

Melissa looked around. "We haven't been on 20,000 Leagues under the Sea yet. Why don't we go there?"

"Oh, yeah, that's right. OK, we'll go on that one next."

They waited in a long line, then climbed into the small submarine together.

"This is probably as close as you'll ever get to diving, since you won't learn to swim," Tyree teased Melissa.

After everybody got in, a loud tinny voice—the submarine's invisible captain—announced that they were getting ready to dive. Melissa settled back comfortably in her seat. At least this ride didn't look very scary. They'd probably just see a bunch of fake fish and stuff.

A loud horn sounded. A big burst of bubbles rushed up past the windows. Suddenly, the submarine tilted forward. Melissa's eyes grew wide. Were they really moving? She couldn't tell.

When the bubbles cleared, she looked out the porthole beside her. She was amazed to see what appeared to be an undersea world.

"Cool," Ismael said. "Look at those divers over there! And look at that octopus!"

Two plastic "men" in yellow diving suits were looking at a clump of plastic seaweed; the octopus had its long tentacles wrapped around a small shark. Nearby, a crab and turtle scuttled along the sandy ocean bottom, and a brightly colored fish swam past, almost brushing against the submarine.

"Wow," said Melissa. "This is fun."

The horn sounded, and they dived again. This time, when the bubbles cleared, the scene was a little scarier. Creepy music started playing inside the submarine. A black eel slithered out of some rocks and headed toward a diver. A huge shark chomped a fish in its sharp, pointed teeth. Melissa stared, her eyes wide. Never, ever, in a billion years would she swim in water around things like that! The whole idea gave her shivers. She was just glad the shark and eel weren't real.

The rest of the day passed quickly. That night, they watched the big fireworks show over Cinderella's Castle. It filled the night sky with dazzling bursts of color and light.

"This is my best Fourth of July ever." Melissa sighed, gazing up at the popping fireworks. "Thanks a lot for bringing all of us along, Titi."

"I'm glad you're having fun," said Aunt Delia. "But remember, we've still got lots more stuff to do. Wet 'n' Wild, then Daytona Beach and Universal Studios . . . you're going to be worn out before you get back home."

"I like getting worn out. As long as it's not at school, anyway."

A DAY TO RELAX

The next day, after a good night's sleep, the adults got up early. They decided to go to the grocery store to buy toothpaste and a few other things they'd forgotten to pack. Uncle Willy woke Tyree and the other kids to see if they wanted to go along.

"I'd rather stay here," Tyree said. "There's a big pool downstairs."

Melissa yawned, still too sleepy to think straight. "I'm too tired right now to go anywhere. You guys go ahead. We'll be OK."

Aunt Delia shrugged. "OK. You older kids just make sure to keep an eye on Stacy and Wiwie if you go swimming. We'll be back in a little while, and then we can all get some breakfast."

As soon as they left, Tyree sat up and dug around in his suitcase until he found his bathing suit. "Let's go down to the pool. We can swim till they get back."

Melissa stretched lazily. "All right. But don't you push me in. I don't want to get my hair wet."

Tyree and Ismael looked at each other and rolled their eyes. Girls!

They took turns changing in the bathroom, then all six kids trooped out of the room together, carrying their towels. Giovanni wanted to ride the elevator all the way up to the top floor, so they did that first. The ride made Melissa feel a little sick.

She was glad when the elevator doors opened at the bottom floor to let them out.

They played in the pool for a half hour, laughing and splashing. Tyree swam up behind Melissa and grabbed both her ankles. When she squealed, Tyree bobbed to the surface with a gleeful grin.

"Shark!" he teased. "Look out, Melissa, here comes another one!"

"Quit, it Papito!" she said, splashing him. "I don't like things grabbing me underwater."

"What'd you think it was, a *pool* shark?" Tyree snickered. "I hear they're really bad this time of year."

They swam for another half hour, then decided they were starving. Where *were* all the adults? They said they would only be gone a few minutes!

"Why don't we just order breakfast from room service?" Tyree suggested. "That way we don't have to wait for them to get back before we eat."

"Good idea," said Melissa. "Let's do it."

They were waiting for the elevator when Tyree suddenly slapped his forehead. "The key! Did any of you remember to bring the room key?"

Melissa and Ismael exchanged startled looks. "I know I didn't," Melissa said. "Did you, Ismael?"

"Nope."

"Great," Tyree said in disgust. "Now we're locked out." He thought, then snapped his fingers. "I've got it. Why don't we order room service at the counter, then get the hotel people to give us another key? That should work."

Wrapped in soggy towels, they dripped their

way over to the counter. After explaining what had happened, they rattled off a list of the food they wanted for breakfast. It ended up being an awful lot of food.

"You're sure it's OK with your parents for you to order all this stuff?" the girl behind the desk asked.

"Sure," Tyree said. "They said we'd go out to eat as soon as they got back, but they're taking too long. We've worked up an appetite."

"OK. I'll send a janitor upstairs with you to let you back into your rooms. Your food will be up in a few minutes."

Walking into the room, Melissa shivered; the air conditioning was turned to maxi-freeze! She snatched up some dry clothes and ran for the bathroom. "I get to change first!" she yelled.

Breakfast was delivered a few minutes later: plates and plates filled with eggs and bacon and toast and sausage. They were eating and watching TV when a key turned in the lock. Aunt Delia and the other adults were back.

They walked in and stopped, staring in surprise at all the food. "Hey, where'd you get all this stuff?" Uncle Willy asked.

"Room service," replied Stacy, happily crunching a piece of toast. "We got hungry."

Aunt Delia looked around at all the plates. "How much did it cost?"

Ismael shrugged. "Nothing. Tyree just told them to charge it to our rooms."

"You guys were gone a long time, and we were

all starving," Tyree said sternly. "You said you were just going to the grocery store!"

Aunt Delia bit her lip to hide a smile. "We were, but we decided to stop a few other places." She looked at Uncle Joey and shrugged. "I guess this is what we get for being late!"

That day, the kids hung around the hotel and played in the pool while the adults explored Orlando. They went to bed late and slept in the next day. They planned to spend that whole day at Wet 'n' Wild.

"I'm taking my video camera along again," Aunt Haydee said as they got ready to go the next morning. "That's my excuse for not going on all those water slides."

"Oh, come on," Melissa said. "You won't have any fun like that!"

"Sure I will. I'm going to film all of you while you're screaming and looking like drowned rats. That'll be enough fun for me!"

WET 'N' WILD

It was a bright, hot day, perfect for Wet 'n' Wild. Tyree, Ismael, and Giovanni headed straight for the tallest slides. Melissa decided to stay with Stacy and Wiwie and avoid the rides that had deep water at the end.

Uncle Willy finally decided to go down one of the big slides with the older boys. "If I don't come up at the end, you better jump in and save me," he told his wife.

Aunt Haydee laughed. "Sorry, but I'll be filming the whole thing. It would get my camera wet."

Uncle Willy followed Tyree and the others to the top. When it was his turn, he sat down, took a deep breath, and launched himself down the slide.

Aunt Haydee kept her camera pointed right at him the whole time. She filmed him as he shot down the steep slide, his mouth open in a happy scream. She filmed him as he splashed into the deep pool at the bottom. She filmed him as he sank like a rock to the bottom.

Uncle Willy waved his arms and legs around like a crazy octopus, his cheeks puffed out. Aunt Haydee was laughing so hard she could barely hold the camera straight.

"Come on, Willy!" she finally shouted. "Quit fooling around!"

It wasn't until the Wet 'n' Wild lifeguard dived in and pulled Uncle Willy out, coughing and sputtering, that Aunt Haydee realized he really had been drowning. She put the camera down and patted him on the back.

"Why didn't you do something?" Uncle Willy yelled after he caught his breath. "I almost drowned!"

"I thought you were kidding around," Aunt Haydee said. Seeing that he was OK, she added, "At least I got the whole thing on film. If you'd drowned, we could've played it at your funeral."

"Thanks a lot. Remind me to start looking around for a new wife . . . one that doesn't own a video camera."

Back in the hotel room that night, Melissa and Tyree talked excitedly about the next day. They were going to spend a few days at Daytona Beach and then go tour Universal Studios.

"I can't wait to get to the beach," Tyree said. "Maybe I'll go surfing."

"You don't know how to surf!" Melissa retorted.

"How hard can it be? Maybe they rent surfboards there. I'm going to check." He gave Melissa a sideways look. "What are you gonna do, just lay around on the beach trying to keep your hair dry?"

"No, smartie. I'll wade around and stuff. I just don't like going way out where it's over my head."

After a late breakfast the next morning, they packed up their suitcases and piled back into the two vans. The kids, planning to go straight to the beach, put on their swimsuits.

It was about two o'clock when they reached the hotel in Daytona Beach where they had reservations. It looked a little shabby on the outside, but they thought it might be nicer inside.

"We need to hurry now," Aunt Delia said as they checked in. "Uncle Joey and I have some business to take care of here this afternoon. Let's take all our bags upstairs and get settled in. As soon as we get back from our appointment, we'll all go down to the beach together."

"Can't we go now?" Stacy whined.

"No. And from the looks of the pool, I think you'd be better off staying out of it, too. I hope the rooms are nicer than the rest of this place!"

When they got upstairs, though, Aunt Haydee

wrinkled her nose. "It's dirty," she said. "The room even smells bad!" Everybody else crowded in behind her.

"The beds aren't even made!" Melissa said. "Gross! I don't want to sleep on somebody else's dirty old sheets."

Aunt Delia sighed. "This isn't going to work. Look, we have to go now or we'll be late, but as soon as we get back we'll move to another hotel, OK? For now, you guys just stay here and watch TV."

Melissa was disappointed. "How long will you be gone?"

Uncle Joey glanced at his watch. "Probably about two hours. We'll hurry."

Tyree groaned. "Two hours! Maybe we should order room service again."

Aunt Delia laughed. "Don't you dare. Haydee and Willy can go buy snacks if you get hungry. Your little breakfast the other day cost us almost a hundred dollars!"

Melissa, Tyree, Ismael, and Giovanni sat cross-legged on the carpet and played cards while Stacy and Wiwie watched TV and fought over the Game Boy. By the time Aunt Delia and Uncle Joey got back, they were all feeling restless and cooped up.

"Finally!" Tyree said, jumping up. "Can we go to the beach now?"

Aunt Delia nodded wearily. "But first we need to get out of this dump and move over to the other hotel. I already called and got us new rooms. Grab your suitcases and let's go!"

Ten minutes later they trooped into the lobby of

the new hotel, located right on the beach. Even little Stacy was impressed by the difference.

"This is a lot nicer," she murmured. "Can we go look at the pool?"

Uncle Willy nodded. After asking the desk clerk for directions, the kids headed toward the back. Melissa and Tyree were the first ones to burst out onto the patio around the pool.

"Wow!" Melissa said. "Check out the waterfall!"

One end of the pool had a big clump of rocks, made to look like a waterfall. This was *definitely* nicer than the scummy pool at the hotel they'd left.

"Let's see if it's OK for us to jump in since we're already in our swimsuits," Tyree suggested. "We can stay down here while they go upstairs and change."

Aunt Delia said it was fine. With gleeful squeals, the six kids jumped into the pool. Tyree and Giovanni wanted to play "chicken," and Melissa finally agreed—but only if they stayed toward the shallow end of the pool.

They were in the middle of a noisy, laughing game when Aunt Delia, Uncle Joey, Aunt Haydee, and Uncle Willy all came down in swimsuits.

"Come on, kids!" Aunt Haydee called. "We're going down to the beach for a quick swim, then we'll go to dinner."

"Oh, Mommy, do we have to get out now?" Stacy whined. "We're having fun!"

"You can play in the pool more later if you want. Right now you need to hurry. It's almost six o'clock, and you can't go swimming at the beach after dark. It's too dangerous. Come on!"

With lots of grumbles and complaints, the kids got out and toweled themselves off. Still, they *had* all wanted to go to the beach today.

Aunt Delia was carrying a big sheet to spread out on the sand. "I'm just going to lay out and enjoy the sun," she said. "I don't want to get my hair wet."

Melissa shot a triumphant look at Tyree. "Me either. It takes too long to wash and blow-dry. I'm just going to go out a little way and jump over the waves."

"Well, me and Ismael are going to swim," Tyree said. "We don't care if we get our hair wet. What's the fun of going to the beach if you stay dry?"

"You don't *have* any hair," Melissa said. She straightened one of the suspenders on her bathing suit. The suit was made to look like a two-piece, but it was really one. "You shave it all off."

"Maybe you should, too. Then you wouldn't worry so much about getting it wet!"

When they started out onto the sand, Aunt Haydee cupped her hand over her eyes to look up and down the beach. "Boy, the lifeguard towers are sure spaced out a long way here," she said. "Looks like we're kind of right in between them."

Uncle Willy pointed to a sign on one of the posts. "They're off-duty now, anyway. It says they get off at six o'clock. They must've just left."

"Guess you'd better stay out of the water, Uncle Willy," Tyree quipped. "There won't be any lifeguards to save you this time when Aunt Haydee tries to let you drown."

"OK, Papito," Aunt Haydee said with a laugh.

Pretending to be angry, she swatted at him. "You'd better watch it."

DANGER IN THE WAVES

The sun was low, but still hot, forming a bright glare on the water. Swimmers dotted the ocean like bright-colored toys.

Aunt Delia snapped open her sheet and let it drift down onto the sand. "Ah, this is nice," she said, stretching out on it happily. Uncle Joey and Uncle Willy both sat down beside her.

"The waves look kind of high today," Aunt Haydee said. "Just watch them bring in a shark!" She laughed. "I think I'll go out and swim with the kids. Come on, you guys."

Tyree and Ismael raced out into the water and plowed through the waves, yelling and splashing. Giovanni and Aunt Haydee followed, and then Melissa with Stacy and Wiwie.

"Ooh!" Stacy giggled as the salty water rushed over her feet. "It's cold!"

Melissa reached down to take Stacy and Wiwie's hands. "Doesn't the sand feel funny? It's like it washes right out from under your feet."

Melissa led her young cousins out just far enough so the waves came to their waists. Farther out, Tyree and Ismael were splashing and shouting to each other. Stacy waved to Aunt Haydee, and she waved back.

"OK," Melissa said, "now watch for the waves. Right when they get to us, we'll all jump!"

When the next wave rushed up to them, the three of them jumped as high as they could. The wave lifted them up, then sat them back down again. Melissa kept a good grip on both children's hands, afraid they might accidentally get swept away.

"That was fun!" Wiwie said, his face beaming. "Let's do it again!"

They had their backs to the shore, so they didn't see that Uncle Willy had gotten up from the sheet to watch them. He was shading his eyes with one hand.

"Here comes another one!" Melissa said. "Now, *jump!*"

Behind them, Uncle Willy started out into the water. He shouted once, but they couldn't hear him over the roar of the surf. They were getting ready to jump again when they heard a faint call.

"Stacy! Wiwie!"

Melissa turned around, searching the water. After a moment she spotted her uncle wading toward them. Still holding the children's hands, she started back to meet him.

"Those waves are getting too high," Uncle Willy said when they met him. "I want Stacy and Wiwie to come back up to the beach."

"I don't want to go in!" Wiwie fussed. "We're having fun! Melissa can take care of us!"

"I know, but I'm afraid you'll get knocked down. Come on out. Maybe we can build a sand castle."

He picked up Wiwie in one arm and Stacy in the other. "Are you coming back to the beach now, Melissa?" he asked.

Melissa hesitated. The waves *were* getting kind of high. But Tyree and the others were still out swimming around. She decided she might as well enjoy the water.

"I think I'm going to stay out for just a few more minutes," she said.

As Uncle Willy started back toward the beach, she waded back out. The waves were a little bigger, but they still weren't too bad. Although the crowd had thinned a little, the water was still full of swimmers.

Melissa giggled when she saw Tyree and Giovanni trying to body surf. Aunt Haydee and Ismael were bobbing around in the water next to them. Off to her right, three kids were shrieking with laughter as they tossed a ball back and forth.

Just then a hard, foamy wave started toward Melissa. She tensed, waiting for just the right moment to jump. The trick was to let the water smoothly sweep you up off your feet instead of crashing into you. She liked trying to time it just right.

Closer . . . closer . . . *now*!

With a happy squeal, she kicked off from the sandy ocean bottom. But at that very instant, something razor sharp clamped down on her right leg, holding her down. The wave slammed into her, filling her mouth with salty water. She was still sputtering when something jerked her all the way under the murky green water.

The first shock left her frozen, unable to move or even think. The greeny-gray seawater was clouded with stirred-up sand; she couldn't see two inches in front of her face. It wasn't until her right cheek scraped something rough that she realized she was being dragged along the bottom by her leg—out toward deeper water.

The thought snapped her out of her frozen state. With a water-choked scream, she clawed at the sand with both hands and then doubled her left leg under her. She pushed up from the bottom with a mighty heave. But something still had hold of her right leg, pinning her down. Her face barely broke the surface. Seawater poured into her mouth as she gasped for air.

"Help!" she shrieked. "Papito, help me!" Her voice was high and choked. She didn't know if her cousin heard her. Panicked, she peered down through the water—then shrieked again.

A huge shark had her right leg clamped in its jaws!

"No!" she gasped in terror. The sleek, shadowy creature was as long as a couch; its tail, far off to her left, was barely visible through the foamy seawater. As she stared down in horror, it worked its jaw to get a tighter grip on her leg, then whipped its head viciously from side to side, shaking her like a dog shaking a sock. Melissa screamed and thrashed wildly, trying to pull her leg free.

But she might as well have tried to fight a freight train. The shark was too powerful, too big. She could see its rows of sharp, pointed teeth, and the slit-like gills along the side of its head. It was like a nightmare, only she knew in her heart it was real. *I'm going to die*, she thought hysterically. *It's going to drag me under and eat me. I'll never see my family again.*

Another wave hit her, almost knocking her down. Melissa felt dizzy and faint. Maybe, she thought weakly, it would be better just to let everything go black. There was no way she could get away. If she blacked out, at least she wouldn't know what was happening.

But then Melissa shook herself. She couldn't just give up like that. There had to be something she could do!

With an angry scream, she started beating at the water with her fists. She also used her good leg to kick at the shark's side. She fought and clawed at the shadowy monster, refusing even to think about her leg. She knew it was cut, but she was afraid to know how badly.

The shark's grey-blue skin felt rough, like sandpaper. Melissa kicked it again and again. It didn't even seem to feel it.

Maybe, she thought, if she could just hit it on the nose. Or in the eye . . . maybe it would let go. She drew up her left leg and brought her heel down, hard, on the shark's nose. She felt the solid *thud* of the blow, even underwater.

Instantly, a great weight lifted from her leg. The shark had finally let go!

Heart pounding, Melissa stared down into the water, trying to see where it had gone. It was almost worse not being able to see it anymore. She was terrified that it would simply grab her again from a different direction.

Suddenly, the shark's huge blue-grey tail rose from the water beside her, towering over her like some kind of sea serpent. Melissa screamed in terror and covered her face. The tail slammed down again with a mighty splash, knocking her backward. The shark shot away toward the open sea.

Melissa splashed back up again, grabbing her bleeding leg with both hands.

"Shark!" she screamed. "*Shark!*"

THE RESCUE

Tyree, Ismael, and Giovanni were still bodysurfing when a high, piercing scream made them look back toward shore. Melissa had been playing in the waves, laughing and squealing with each one. But this time her voice sounded different—they could hear the terror in her voice.

Tyree squinted, trying to see better. It looked like Melissa was holding her leg. His first thought was that she'd been stung by a jellyfish.

"Hey, I think a jellyfish got Melissa! Let's go see what's the matter."

"Maybe it's an octopus!" Giovanni said excitedly. They started toward Melissa. Aunt Haydee, alerted by Melissa's screams, was also swimming toward her.

"What's the matter?" Tyree asked as he got closer.

"Shark!" Melissa sobbed. "Look out, there's a shark! It bit my leg!"

Tyree's mouth flew open. He whirled around,

looking at the water, but he didn't see a triangle fin. Then he saw Melissa's leg—and gasped. A deep, moon-shaped gash ran from her thigh all the way down to below her knee. Her leg looked like it was almost bitten off.

"Oh, man!" Tyree said. "Ismael, you and Giovanni go get help, quick!"

Aunt Haydee swam up just then. She took one horrified look at Melissa's leg, then clapped her hands over her niece's eyes.

"Don't look," she said. "Come on, Papito, help me get her to shore."

"I've already seen it!" Melissa shouted. She pushed her aunt's hand away. "A shark grabbed my leg and kept biting at it. I kicked him in the nose until he finally let go."

While Melissa pressed on her leg to stop the bleeding, Aunt Haydee and Tyree dragged her through the water toward the shore as fast as they could. Many people, unaware of the danger, were still swimming and playing.

"Get out of the water!" Tyree yelled repeatedly. "There's a shark! Get out!" Those who heard him quickly started toward the beach.

Giovanni and Ismael were just reaching the shore. They ran up to Aunt Delia and Uncle Willy, yelling and waving their arms. By the time Melissa got there, Giovanni was already racing down the beach looking for a lifeguard. They had all gone off duty less than twenty minutes before.

Aunt Delia ran up to Melissa, her face pale. "Are you all right?"

"A shark bit me," Melissa said weakly. She

moved her hand away from her leg. Aunt Delia stared, then burst into hysterical tears. Melissa felt herself slipping into panic again. "Get away from me, Titi!" she cried. "I don't need that right now!"

Uncle Willy scooped Melissa up. He carried her over to the sheet and laid her down, then squeezed her hand.

"You're going to be fine," he said. "They're calling an ambulance now. Just stay calm."

Melissa was glad to have Uncle Willy there. He had always been like a father to her. "Don't leave me," she begged.

"I won't," her uncle assured her. "Don't worry."

Soon the beach was crowded with swimmers. At first they were curious to hear about the shark attack. But after a few minutes, many of them grew bored—and went right back out into the water. Melissa couldn't understand it.

"Are they crazy?" she said. "That thing's still out there somewhere!" She looked over at Stacy and Wiwie. "I'm just glad it didn't happen to one of them, Uncle Willy. If you hadn't come out and gotten them . . ."

"Don't think about it," he said firmly. "It's all over now."

An ambulance arrived a few minutes later and took Melissa to the hospital. She was in surgery for a little more than an hour.

When she woke up, the doctor told her he'd removed three shark teeth from her leg. He asked if she wanted to keep them as souvenirs.

Melissa shuddered. "No!" she told him. "I don't even want to see them."

Tyree was disgusted when he heard about the teeth. He was visiting Melissa in her hospital room.

"I can't believe you," he said. "If you didn't want the shark teeth, I'd have taken them! That's so cool—he left his teeth right in your leg!"

"Leave me alone, Papito, or I'll leave *my* teeth in *your* leg!" Melissa snapped. "Why do boys always have to be so gross?"

"Hey, don't I deserve a reward for getting you back up to the beach? Not to mention that I almost starved to death sitting in the hospital while you were operated on. I never did get any dinner, you know." He grinned wickedly. "We didn't get to eat, but I guess the shark did, right?"

Melissa groaned and put a pillow over her face. "Go away, Papito. You're disgusting."

As soon as Melissa was allowed to leave the hospital, the whole family drove back home to New York. Aunt Delia and Uncle Joey decided that maybe they'd try another honeymoon the next year.

"One with less sharks," Uncle Joey joked. "And less kids!"

Later, Melissa learned that a shark expert had looked at the teeth taken from her leg. He thought they were from a tiger shark. From their size, the shark must have been about eight feet long, more than big enough to carry off a small twelve-year-old. Melissa had probably saved her life by kicking it in the nose.

Melissa also learned that it is never a good idea to swim in the ocean around dark—feeding time for sharks. It also isn't wise to swim around schools of small bait fish. A hungry shark could easily mistake a person for a nice, juicy fish!

"Still," Melissa said to Tyree a few weeks later, "why did it swim past you and Ismael and everybody else just to bite me?"

Tyree grinned. "It was probably scared of us. It knew how tough we were. It was afraid we would beat it up."

"Oh, right. You probably would've fainted and gotten eaten. Not a bad idea, come to think of it."

The attack left Melissa with a big scar on her right leg, and she had nightmares for a while. But it also showed her that she was a lot tougher than she'd ever thought. The day she faced the shark, she hadn't fainted or quit. She had ignored her fear, used her head, and fought back with all her strength.

And, as she liked to point out to Tyree, she had *won*!

Melissa Rodriquez recovers from the shark attack to her leg.

A Ski Slope Rescue!

THE SHAWN DURRANT STORY

ABOVE: Shawn Durrant and his prized truck.

Shawn peered hopefully into the kitchen cabinet. He was hungry for a late-night snack, but he didn't feel like cooking anything. He searched the shelves, then sighed. It looked like cereal again.

He pulled out a box and shook it. "Shredded hay?" he muttered. "I don't think I'm *that* hungry."

He shoved it back and grabbed another box. It held brownish oat lumps that looked a lot like dog food. He fished out a lump, smelled it, then popped it in his mouth. Not bad.

Rags, the family mutt, was sprawled half asleep on the kitchen floor. The minute Shawn started toward the table, the dog scrambled to his feet. He stared up at the boy licking his dog lips hungrily and wagging his tail.

"OK, OK," Shawn said, fishing out another oat lump and tossing it to Rags. "Check it out—Purina People Chow!"

Rags gave it one curious sniff, then ignored it. The teenager laughed.

"It figures," he said. "I bet your dog food has more flavor than this stuff. I wouldn't eat it either if I could find anything else."

He poured a bowl of cereal and plopped down at the table with a sigh. His after-school job at a nearby ski resort had left him drained. He felt like he could sleep for about forty hours.

He had just taken his first big bite when his dad shuffled in. Mr. Durrant was a mechanic who taught diesel repair at the local Job Corps. Right now, though, his thin brown hair was sticking up and he was wearing an old blue bathrobe.

"Hi, son," he said. He grabbed a bowl and spoon and joined Shawn at the table. "How'd it go at work tonight? Anything exciting happen?"

"Not really," Shawn replied. He covered a yawn, then rubbed the tip of his slightly crooked nose. "I'm still learning how to run the ski lifts and everything, but it's really not hard. I think I just stayed out too late over the weekend with Bryan and the guys. I need some sleep."

"Rough life, being a teenager," Mr. Durrant said with a smile.

Shawn grinned. "OK, Dad, give it a rest." He scooped up another spoonful of cereal. "Oh," he said suddenly, "I just remembered. There *was* one exciting thing that happened tonight. On my way home, an ambulance came screaming up behind me. It must have been going about ninety. I slowed way down and tried to squeeze as far over as I could, but there was nowhere to stop. Anyway, it had just passed me when it swerved and scraped a telephone pole along the side of the road. The back doors of the ambulance popped open."

Mr. Durrant stopped chewing. "You're kidding! What happened?"

"Well, there was a guy, or maybe it was a woman, on the bed inside, and two paramedics working on him. Or her. Anyway, whoever it was had bandages wrapped all around their head like a mummy."

"Good grief. Did they fall out?"

"No, no, nothing like that. One of the paramedics grabbed the doors real quick and slammed them shut again. But before he got them closed a bunch of stuff blew out. It was mostly papers, but there was also some kind of flat metal box, maybe about the size of a small tool box. It bounced on the road and almost hit my truck."

Mr. Durrant shook his head. "Did they stop to pick it up?"

"No. I don't think they even knew it fell out. They just kept going. But I thought it might be important, so I thought I'd better stop and find it."

"Good idea. What was in it?"

"Well, it was dark, so it took me a few minutes to find it. It had rolled off into the grass and kind of under a bush. Anyway, I finally found it, and I took it over to the truck where I could see better. It wasn't locked or anything, so I opened it."

"What was in it?"

"You wouldn't believe it. There were some *body parts* inside!"

"What?"

"I mean it. The very first thing I saw was a plastic baggie-thing with a whole *toe* in it!"

Mr. Durrant dropped his spoon with a clank. He stared at his son, open-mouthed. "No! You didn't touch it, did you?"

"No way! But I knew I had to get it back to the hospital right away. So I called a toe truck."

There was a long pause, then Mr. Durrant blinked. "A tow truck?"

"A *toe* truck," Shawn said clearly, a big grin spreading across his face. "You know, a T-O-E truck!" He slapped the table and leaned back in his chair, laughing and pointing at his father. "Boy, I sure got you on that one! You should see your face!"

Mr. Durrant groaned. "I can't believe I fell for that. I should've known better."

Shawn was pleased with himself. "Sometimes I crack myself up. Do you know how old that story is?"

"You just caught me half asleep," said Mr. Durrant with dignity. "Now if you'd tried that in the morning—"

"You'd still have fallen for it," Shawn interrupted. "You always do." Still smiling, he scooped up a soggy oat lump. "But listen, now that you're all nice and awake—"

"Hey, wait a minute. First you play a dirty trick on me, then you want to ask a favor?"

"Not a big one. Well, not a *really* big one. It's just about my truck. I need some advice. Rowdy keeps bugging me to race him, but we both know his Chevy's a lot faster than my Ford. I want to make my truck faster. If I save up enough to build a bigger engine, will you help me put it in?"

Shawn knew his dad liked talking about engines and things almost as much as he did. His truck was a jacked-up 1979 Ford, painted red and grey. Shawn practically lived in it anytime he wasn't at school or work.

"I think I could probably do that," Mr. Durrant said, glad to leave the subject of "toe" trucks. "What did you have in mind?"

They munched cereal as they talked, both of them enjoying the company. Since Shawn had started working nights at the Nordic Valley Ski Resort in Utah's Wasatch Mountains, he didn't get to see his dad as much. Sometimes he missed him. They had always been closest when they were working together on cars and trucks.

NIGHT SHIFT AT NORDIC VALLEY

The next night when Shawn went to work, he told his partner, Phil, about the joke he'd played on his father.

"It was great," he said, rubbing his gloved hands together to get warm. They were crunching through the snow toward the ski lift they'd be running that night. "He was sure I'd found a human toe beside the road!"

Phil laughed, his breath making a cloud in the icy air. "That's pretty good," he agreed. Like Shawn, he had only been working at Nordic Valley a few weeks. Since they both had to spend hours each night in the freezing cold and wind, they were dressed alike in heavy parkas and rubber boots.

Nordic Valley had two ski lifts. The lifts were open-air rides that hauled skiers up the hills. Seats dangled from metal cables strung along tall posts, like telephone poles; at the top and bottom of each hill the chairs dipped close to the ground so people could get on and off. The main lift, on the steepest hill, also had an area where skiers could get off halfway up.

Shawn had always loved working outside, even when it was cold. In the few weeks he'd been at Nordic Valley he had already learned a lot about the lifts. He liked the main lift best, where he and Phil would be working tonight. The skiers there all knew what they were doing, so they didn't need much help. He and Phil would mostly be there in case of an emergency.

The "bunny" lift, on the easy hill used by beginners and young children, was a lot more work. Shawn had only run that lift twice. It made him nervous to load little kids into the chairs, even though he wedged them in beside their parents. You never knew what they might do, especially when they suddenly found themselves swinging forty feet above the ground! If one of them ever tumbled out onto the hard-packed snow, it would be like hitting concrete.

"Good thing we're not on the bunny lift tonight," Shawn said aloud. "On family night, it's always packed with kids."

"I haven't worked that one yet," Phil said. "Have you?"

"Yeah, just a couple times. I just don't like hassling with kids. They do stupid things."

"I know what you mean. Well, it shouldn't be too bad for us tonight. Not as many people out as usual."

Shawn nodded. "It's probably the wind. People are crazy to get out in this if they don't have to!"

When they reached the main lift, Shawn went to the control panel and turned it on. Slowly, the cable overhead started moving. A few skiers, seeing it start up, headed their way.

Shawn quickly checked to make sure everything was working all right. High winds could blow the cable off its track, leaving the chairs stuck in midair. If that ever happened when people were on the lift, he was supposed to use a special rescue platform to get them down. The thought made him uneasy. He had never liked heights, and he sure wouldn't like to climb up there when the wind was howling like this. He hoped nothing like that ever happened while he was on duty.

The first skiers lined up, waiting to get on the lift. When Shawn waved for them to go ahead, a woman inched forward. Phil stood nearby as a chair glided up behind her. She quickly slid into it and held on, letting it scoop her off her feet and sweep her upward. One by one the others slid into chairs and followed her up, their legs and skis dangling.

Shawn stayed near the controls, watching, but nothing exciting happened. An icy gust swirled loose snow in a little tornado around his feet. He rubbed at his face with his gloved hands. Even though his nose was crooked, he didn't want it to freeze off. It was the only one he had.

He waited until the last skier was safely on the lift, then turned to Phil. "I'm going inside the hut for a minute to warm up, OK? It's bad out here tonight. My nose feels like an ice cube."

Phil's muffler was pulled up until only his eyes showed. "No joke. I think my eyeballs are frozen. Hurry up, though. They'll all be back down in a few minutes."

The wooden hut near the lift was really a storage shed, but at least it was out of the wind. Shawn ducked inside, then sighed with relief. It felt about twenty degrees warmer. He stamped his feet and rubbed his arms, trying to thaw out.

When he saw through the window that another group of skiers was lining up, though, he ran back outside.

"OK, it'll be your turn next," he said, patting Phil on the back. "Let's load this group, then I'll babysit for a while."

"Thanks," Phil muttered through chattering teeth. "I'm about frozen stiff."

A few minutes later, Shawn grinned as his partner stumbled over to the shack and disappeared inside, slamming the door. It was going to be another long, cold night—and then they'd have to do it all over again the next day! Good thing he liked his job. Even though it was cold, it beat his last two jobs: flipping burgers and working in a warehouse.

BIG BROTHER, LITTLE SISTER

The next few days passed quickly. Between school, work, and friends, Shawn didn't spend much time at home. He breezed in after school every day, grabbed some food, maybe watched TV for a few minutes, then took off again with Bryan or Rowdy. If he hung around the house too long his brother and sister got on his nerves.

Especially Jeremiah, Shawn thought as he left the house on Friday afternoon. His brother was fifteen, but he tried to act like he was twenty. All he wanted to talk about was girls or guns, his two favorite hobbies. Shawn loved his brother, but they usually ended up fighting.

Celeste, seven, wasn't so bad, but she always pestered him to take her places. Maybe that was why he didn't like running the bunny lift. He went to work to get *away* from kids, not to see more of them!

He ended up working that Saturday, and then spent the rest of the weekend running around with Bryan. By late Sunday afternoon, though, Shawn was starting to feel a little guilty about ignoring his family. Jeremiah wouldn't care, but Celeste still kind of looked up to him. He decided to drop in at home for a surprise visit.

When he walked into the living room, his sister jumped up with a big grin. With her blond hair and blue eyes, she looked like a little angel. She ran over to hug him.

"Shawn!" she said. "Where've you been?"

Shawn patted her on the head. "I'm a busy man. What have you been up to, Sis?"

Celeste flapped her hand toward her friend, six-year-old Joee, who was sprawled out on the couch. "Me and Joee have just been sitting around watching TV. It's been really boring."

"I bet. Where's everybody else?"

"I dunno. I think Mom went to the grocery store. Jeremiah's out with his friends. And I think Dad's in the garage."

"Hm. Well, since everybody else is busy, how would you feel about going out to see a movie or something with me?"

Celeste's eyes opened wide. "Sure! But can Joee come, too?"

Shawn pretended to think about it. Since he had already decided to act noble, though, he might as well go all the way.

"Sure, why not?" he said. "That way you'll be able to giggle twice as loud."

"Thanks! Come on, Joee, let's go call your mom. My brother's taking us to the movies!"

As they ran off, Shawn sank into his dad's recliner. This, he thought wryly, would be his good deed for the week. He hoped God was watching.

Soon Celeste and Joee charged back in, ready to go. They skipped out to Shawn's truck, climbed into it, and started bouncing up and down on the seat. Shawn shook his head. He hadn't even started the engine yet, and they were already having fun. Little kids were weird.

"OK," he said after they settled down. "Here are

the rules. First, I want you both to put on your seat belts and sit still while I'm driving. And when we get to the theater, I don't want you wandering off while I'm buying tickets. You're both pretty cute, and somebody might want to steal you."

He smiled. "Course, as soon as they got to know you they'd want to bring you right back, but by then it might be too late."

"Shawn!" Celeste said indignantly. "That wasn't very nice!"

"What do you mean?" Shawn said, pretending not to understand. "I said you were cute, didn't I?"

"The other part. About bringing us back."

"Oh." Shawn started the truck and backed out of the driveway. "Well, anyway, you guys need to stay right with me. If you have to go to the bathroom or anything, you'll have to wait and go together."

Celeste and Joee looked at each other and rolled their eyes. What did he think they were, four years old?

The movie wasn't all that great, but they had fun anyway. On the way home, they stopped to get ice cream cones. All in all, Shawn thought, the evening hadn't been too bad. Still, he was glad to get home and let Celeste and Joee tumble back out of his truck. Their giggling had almost made him glad the next day was Monday. Compared to an evening of baby-sitting, a full day of algebra and ski lifts seemed easy.

But the next night, when Shawn pulled into the parking lot at Nordic Valley, the first thing he saw was a stream of parents with little kids getting out of their cars. He groaned. It was Monday: family night!

On the way inside he silently prayed that he wouldn't get stuck with the bunny lift. He had already done his good deed for the week. He wasn't in any mood to deal with a bunch of runny-nosed little kids.

When he checked the work schedule, though, he and Phil were both assigned to the bunny lift. Shawn gritted his teeth. If he'd had the job a little longer he might have asked his boss to change it, but it was too soon to start griping. What a lousy way to start a new week!

Phil was already outside. "Hey!" he greeted Shawn. "I hear we're doing the kiddie lift tonight."

"You'd better brace yourself. It's a lot more work than the main lift."

It was another cold, windy evening. Shawn pulled his collar up around his neck as they hiked to the bunny hill. Sure enough, there were already a few families waiting. He turned on the lift, then went over to help Phil load the first group.

"It isn't always easy to get kids onto the chairs," he explained. "You have to lift them up onto the seat, then shove them back in beside their mom or dad. If they start fighting or crying, you have to get them back off in a hurry, before the chair takes off."

Shawn helped load the first group of kids, then paused to look around. "Before we get too busy, I want to run over and make sure the hut here is open," he said. "We'll need a place to warm up later."

Phil, bending to lift a little boy into a chair with his mom, nodded. "Go ahead. This isn't too bad."

Shawn trotted over to the wooden building and tugged on the door, but it wouldn't budge. He looked up. More families were moving toward the bunny hill.

"Phil!" he called to his partner. "The hut's locked. I've got to run back up to the lodge to get the key. Can you handle things by yourself for a minute?"

"Sure!" Phil called. "I'm doing OK."

The lodge was in clear sight just up the hill. Shawn started running, his rubber boots slipping on several hard ice patches. He had only gone about forty feet when a faint scream sounded behind him.

DANGER ON THE SKI LIFT

At first he barely noticed it; the wind blowing in his ears and the crunch of his footsteps in the snow blocked out almost everything else. But when the sharp cry sounded a second time, he stopped. It sounded like a child!

Puzzled, Shawn glanced back toward the lift. Kids often laughed and screamed as they skied down the slope, but the bunny lift had just opened. There hadn't been time yet for any of the kids to start back down.

Maybe, he thought, it was just the metal cable scraping against something. He glanced up—then froze. Something pink was dangling down from one of the chairs high overhead. In a flash of horror, Shawn saw that it was a child.

"Oh, no!" he yelled. "Phil, stop the lift! *Stop the lift!*"

In a panic, the teenager raced back down the hill, his eyes glued to the small figure overhead. The child was dangling by one arm, kicking and screaming in terror. The chair was still moving. If it reached the first tall post, it would have to bump over several metal pullies. The jolt, Shawn realized, might shake the child loose.

He had to do something!

Slipping and falling on the ice, Shawn scrambled back down toward the bottom of the lift. As he got closer, he saw that a woman was leaning out of the chair, holding on to the child's sleeve. It was a little girl, dressed in a pink snowsuit and green jacket.

"Help!" the woman screamed. "Help, I'm dropping her!"

Phil finally reached the control panel. In a panic, he jabbed at the emergency stop button. The cable slowly whined to a stop. The mother and daughter were left swinging three stories above the ground.

Shawn ran up and skidded to a halt just beneath the terrified child. Looking up, all he could see was the bottom of two skis and a squirming bundle of pink far overhead.

"Mommy!" the girl wailed. "Help me!"

Shawn had thought at first that he'd be able to catch her if she dropped. But now he realized that she was too high. He'd never be able to break her fall. She would hit the hard snow and be killed.

"Hurry!" the mother screamed in despair. "Please hurry!"

Shawn ran a gloved hand over his face, no longer feeling the cold. Where was everybody else? Where was his boss? He didn't know what to do!

"Hang on, ma'am!" he begged, his mind racing. "Just hang on!"

Suddenly, he remembered the rescue platform. But where was it? Running over to the locked hut, he peered in through the window. If it was in there, he could break the glass and crawl inside to get it.

But the bulky tool wasn't on any of the shelves. Shawn realized it must be in the shed at the top of the hill.

It might as well be on Mars. He could never reach it in time.

Oh, God, he thought, not even realizing he was praying. He glanced around wildly, trying to come up with another plan. If he didn't act soon, the girl would surely die.

Could Phil back the lift down? No, that wouldn't work; the cable only went forward. What about the ski patrol? Shawn's heart gave a hopeful leap, and he looked around. The patrol had rescue tools and trained people who would know just what to do. They would take care of everything.

But for once, the ski patrol was nowhere in sight. Shawn gazed up toward the lodge, wondering if he could get there fast enough to call for them.

"Mom-my!"

The child's frightened wail jolted him into action. By the time the patrol got there, she would have fallen. It was up to him.

"Hold on!" he shouted. "Hold on, I'm coming!"

Still not sure what he was going to do, Shawn sprinted up to the first post. Made of metal, it was over forty feet high. A ladder ran up to the top, where long steel arms stuck out on each side to hold up the cable.

The mother and daughter's chair had stopped about six feet before the post. If Shawn could somehow get close enough to grab the girl . . .

That gave him an idea. "Phil!" he yelled. "Start the lift and run them up to the post! Stop the chair right before they hit it!"

His partner instantly hit the switch. As Shawn started scrambling up the ladder, the overhead cable jerked once, then began to edge upward. If the woman could just hang on for a few more seconds, Shawn would be able to meet her at the top.

Panting, the teenager climbed up two rungs at a time, almost running up the ladder. Above him, he saw the mother peering down over the side of the chair. Her face was pale, her dark eyes wide with shock. Her fist was clenched tightly around the sleeve of her daughter's small jacket.

He was halfway up the ladder when a faint ripping noise sounded above him. The woman gasped.

"Her jacket's coming apart!" she cried. In a lightning-fast move, she used both hands for a moment to grab at the straps on the back of her daughter's ski pants. The chair kept moving upward.

Shawn no longer noticed the icy wind blowing or how his rubber boots kept slipping on the ladder's metal rungs. All he could think about was the little girl plunging down . . . down . . . to slam into the ground below. He *had* to get to her in time!

"Hang on!" he pleaded. "I'm almost there!"

As he lunged up the ladder, the chair overhead crept up to the post—and kept going. From his place down at the controls, Phil couldn't tell exactly when the chair reached the post.

"Phil, *stop*!" Shawn screamed. "You're going too far!"

Phil instantly hit the brake switch, but it took another five seconds for the cable to stop all the way. In that time, the chair climbed another five feet.

Shawn's breath was coming in cold gasps as he clawed his way up the last few rungs to the top. It seemed like he had climbed about nine hundred feet!

His heart sank when he saw how far the chair had gone. There was no way he could reach the girl now from the ladder. Worse yet, if her mother dropped her now, she would have even farther to fall. And it would be his fault.

Another shriek made his heart leap into his throat.

"Her straps are ripping!" the woman screamed. "I'm dropping her!"

Shawn stared helplessly at the sobbing child, dangling from the chair like a broken doll. Her small jacket was bunched up around her head, hiding her face, but several dark curls peeked out against her pink snowsuit. She looked like she could be about Celeste's age.

The thought made Shawn's blood run cold. *Please don't let her fall*, he prayed. *Show me what to do.*

The frantic mother was trying to stretch one leg down to the girl. "Grab onto Mommy's leg, Angie!" she said. "Try to grab my leg!"

But the girl's bunched-up coat had her arms securely pinned. "I can't!" she cried. "Mommy, I'm scared!"

At that moment a strong gust of wind slammed into Shawn, making him grip the ladder tighter. He glanced down nervously. It was a mistake. Seeing the ground forty feet below made him feel weak and dizzy.

COURAGEOUS RESCUE

Ever since he was a little kid, Shawn had been scared of heights. Even when his family had visited the Space Needle, a fancy restaurant at the top of a tower, he had been afraid to look out the window. Looking down always made him feel dizzy.

He shuddered. This was his worst nightmare. He could take anything but this. But unless he was willing to sit back and let the little girl die, Shawn realized he would have to get over his fear. He had to do something—fast!

Shawn shook himself to regain control and

forced his eyes back up. *OK*, he told himself. *Just calm down and think*. There had to be some way for him to get to the girl quickly.

The post's steel arm was just above him. Shawn followed it with his eyes out to where it met the cable. If he could climb out to the cable, he might be able to pull himself, hand over hand, up to the stranded chair. It wasn't a very good plan, but it was the only one he could think of.

There was another ripping sound, followed by the mother's panic-stricken screams. Shawn took a deep breath.

"I'm coming out there to you!" he called, his voice shaking. "Just hold on!"

As he reached up to grab the steel beam, he noticed that his gloved hands were shaking, too. The metal was cold and slippery, coated with ice and snow. One wrong move would send him tumbling off into space.

Shawn quickly shoved the thought aside. Using both hands, he pulled himself up onto the narrow beam, then wrapped his legs around it to keep his balance. The cold wind made his eyes water. He blinked, wanting to see clearly. The next part would be tough.

The arm leading out to the cable was only four or five feet long. But out at the end, where the cable hooked on, there were a bunch of pullies sticking up. By the time he crawled over all that mess to ease himself down to the cable, it might be too late. Every second counted now.

He would have to walk out to the end, then jump for the cable. It was the only way.

The thought of jumping six feet across the forty-foot drop left Shawn's mouth dry. He swallowed but didn't hesitate. If it had to be done, he might as well do it fast.

He brought his feet up onto the beam, then stood up slowly, holding his arms out like a tightrope walker. His rubber boots felt thick and clumsy, but he couldn't do anything about that. He just hoped they wouldn't slip.

Heart pounding, he started forward. With each step, he kicked snow off the slippery beam. He tried to pretend that he was walking along a wall or a ledge, anything that wasn't high. The wind hit him in short gusts, making him feel like he was going to be blown off. If that happened, he knew he would never be able to grab the beam in time to save himself.

Please help me, he prayed. *I've got to do this. There's nobody else.*

Shawn was halfway across the beam when he heard a man's faint call. One of the skiers farther up on the lift was twisted around in his seat, looking back.

"He's almost there!" the man called back to the young mother. "He'll have her in a second!"

The words gave Shawn new strength. Two more steps, and he was to the cable pullies. He squatted down and held onto them to keep his balance.

Now came the hard part.

To his left, six feet up the cable, the chair with the little girl was swaying in the breeze. What if he missed when he leaped for the cable? It was a long, long way to the ground.

Don't think about it, Shawn told himself firmly. He bunched his legs under him like a frog, trying to judge the distance. Even if he could grab the cable, would he be able to hold on? It looked slick and greasy. He flexed his gloved fingers. What if his hands slipped?

Then it'll be all over, Shawn answered himself. But at least he would have tried. Before he could lose his nerve, he took a deep breath, tensed his legs—and jumped.

HANGING ON

For a long moment, Shawn hung in the air like Superman, arms stretched out in front of him, fingers reaching for the cable. Then the thick metal cable slapped his palms. Heart pounding, Shawn grabbed it and held on. He fought down panic as his body swung violently back and forth in midair. He was squeezing the cable so tight that his wrists hurt.

When he finally stopped swinging, he glanced up the cable. He could see the back of the chair, and the outline of the sobbing woman. He could also hear the little girl's pathetic sobs.

"I'm coming!" he yelled. "Just stay calm!"

Shawn thought about doing a pull-up so he could wrap his legs around the cable, but he didn't know if he had enough strength. At that height, he didn't want to take any chances. He decided to inch his way up to the chair.

Sliding his hands sideways one at a time, he

pulled himself up the steep cable. As he got closer he tried not to wiggle around too much, afraid he might shake the child—Angie?—loose. Whenever his hands slipped backwards on the greasy cable, he just gritted his teeth and tried again.

Before long, Shawn's arms and shoulders were burning from the effort. His thick jacket, bunched up under his arms, made it hard to move, and his rubber boots felt like ten-pound weights. His hands started to shake even harder.

Just keep going, he told himself. *I can do this.* His inner "pep talk" helped as he fought his way up the last few feet.

Finally, after what seemed like forever, Shawn got close enough to swing his legs forward and touch the chair. He eased his feet onto the chair back, then clamped his legs and arms around the tall metal post that hooked onto the cable.

Made it, he thought, panting. He would have loved to stay there and catch his breath, but time was running out. In the chair below, the woman was holding onto the last tattered strap of the little girl's ski pants.

Shawn quickly slid down the metal post like a fireman's pole, then dropped into the seat beside the woman. When she looked up at him, Shawn saw that she was near collapse.

"I can't get her up," she sobbed. "I've tried and tried, but I just can't!"

"I'll help you," Shawn said. "Everything's gonna be all right."

Grabbing the chair with one hand, he leaned out

to reach for the little girl. But due to the steep tilt of the lift, Angie was almost hidden underneath the chair. At that angle, it would have taken a weight-lifter to pull her up with one arm. No wonder her mother hadn't been able to do it!

That thought worried Shawn. Even with both of them, it still might be impossible. But if Celeste was in this situation, he knew he would somehow find the strength. His hand closed around Angie's coat.

"OK, we're going to have to pull her up together," he told the mother. "Let's do it on the count of three. Ready?"

The woman nodded. "OK," Shawn said. "One . . . two . . . *three!*"

As they both pulled, muscles straining, the girl slowly came into view. They quickly dragged her into the seat and wedged her between them.

"Angie!" the mother screamed, flinging both arms around her. "Thank God you're all right!"

For the first time, Shawn got a good look at Angie's face. Her dark eyes were red and puffy from crying, and her cheeks were streaked with tears. But to him, she still looked like a little angel.

"I'm glad you're OK," he said, reaching over awkwardly to pat her arm. Still sobbing, she buried her face in her mother's coat. Shawn knew how she felt. His heart was still going ninety miles an hour.

Angie's mother, whose name turned out to be Chris, leaned over and hugged Shawn so hard she almost strangled him.

"Thank you," she said, still barely able to talk. "Thank you for saving her!" Shawn was embarrassed.

"I'm glad I was able to help," he mumbled.

A HUMBLE HERO

Now that the ordeal was all over, Shawn felt kind of strange. He twisted around in his seat to look back down the hill.

"Hey, Phil!" he yelled to his partner. "Go ahead and start the lift now, and run us up to the top!"

Phil waved. A moment later, the lift came to life. Shawn kept his arm around Angie as the chair glided smoothly up the hill.

A small crowd had gathered at the top. Shawn jumped off the seat and then helped Angie get off. He was surprised to find that his legs felt weak and rubbery.

A woman in the crowd stepped forward. "That was a very brave thing you did there, young man. You could have been killed!"

Shawn didn't need her to remind him of that. He could still feel his blood rushing. "It wasn't that big a deal," he muttered. "I was just doing my job."

When the crowd thinned a few minutes later, Shawn was still feeling weak. He walked over to the hut to talk to the guy who worked at the top of the lift.

"Listen, can I switch with you for the rest of the night? I don't think I'm up to going back down there and loading kids the rest of the night."

"Sure, no problem," the worker said. "After all that you deserve a break!"

It was almost eleven o'clock when Shawn got home that night. He felt like a tired, old man as he got out of his truck and shuffled inside. His heart had finally stopped pounding after about two hours, but the excitement had left him exhausted.

Rags greeted him at the door, bouncing around and whining to be petted. Shawn squatted down and scratched his ears. "You know, Rags," he said in a friendly tone, "someday I'm going to get a *real* dog. You're just a useless little mop, you know that?"

Rags beat the floor with his tail and licked Shawn's hand. He didn't care what people said as long as they sounded friendly and kept his food bowl filled.

Shawn sighed and stood up. He wanted to go to bed, but he also wanted a snack, as usual. He paused. Was he hungrier than he was sleepy? In the end, food won out. He wandered into the kitchen and poured a bowl of cereal.

A few minutes later Mr. Durrant walked in. Shawn sometimes wondered if he had cereal radar or something.

"Hi, son," he said, as usual. "How was your day?"

"Pretty good," Shawn said. He hesitated. "I'm not sure, but I think I might have saved a little girl's life tonight."

Mr. Durrant gave him a sideways look. "Oh, really? What did you do, call a *toe* truck?"

Shawn laughed. "No, Dad, I'm serious. I had to

work the bunny lift tonight, and a little girl fell out of a chair. She looked like she was about Celeste's age. I guess she wasn't in the seat very well, so when it started up she slipped out. Her mom grabbed her coat, so she was just dangling there. I had to climb up about forty feet and grab her."

"Really? That sounds pretty scary. You've never liked heights much."

"Yeah. Well, at first I kept hoping somebody else was going to do something. The snow was packed down hard tonight, so I knew if she fell she would be dead. But nobody else was around. Then I started thinking, what if that was Celeste up there? I'd want somebody to help her. So I just did it. It took me a couple of hours to calm down afterward, though."

"I bet." Mr. Durrant gave him a serious look. "Sounds like you're a hero, son. Congratulations."

Shawn flushed. "I wasn't any big hero, Dad. I was scared to death the whole time. I just kept kind of praying the whole time. I think it might've helped."

Mr. Durrant nodded. "I wouldn't be surprised. But I'm still proud of what you did. It wouldn't have done much good to pray for her if you hadn't gone and helped her, now would it?"

"I guess not."

They both munched in silence. Finally, Shawn shoved his bowl away. He leaned back in his chair to give his dad a humorous look.

"Well," he said, "if you think I'm some kind of big hero, maybe you'd like to find some way to reward me?"

Mr. Durrant smiled but didn't answer. Shawn flashed him an impish grin. "So," he continued, "I guess this might be the perfect time to ask you about those new oversize tires I've been wanting for my truck."

Shawn Durrant, rescuer at Nordic Valley Ski Resort, was awarded the Carnegie Medal for Heroism in 1990.

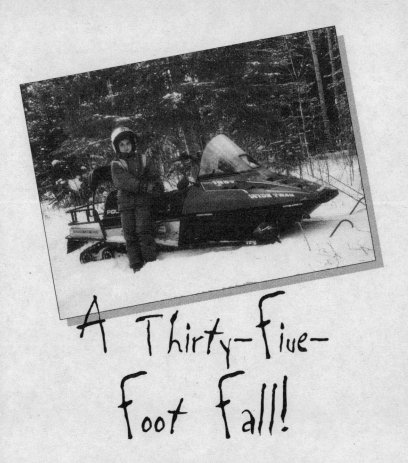

A Thirty-Five-Foot Fall!

THE JOLENE DANIELS STORY

ABOVE: Jolene Daniels with her dad's snowmobile in the bush near her house.

Chantelle, nine, tiptoed along the deck outside her friend's treehouse, listening for whispers or footsteps. All she could hear was the cold wind whistling through the snow-covered branches. She shivered, then glanced back over her shoulder. Where were they? She crept up to peek around the door.

"Chantelle!" squealed a voice right behind her.

The nine-year-old gasped. She whirled around just in time to see her friend, Jolene Daniels, disappearing around the corner. Giggling, Chantelle took off after her.

The treehouse in the Daniels' yard was a favorite hang-out for the neighborhood kids. It was a lot bigger than most treehouses. It had two doors, and an outside deck that went almost all the way around. It also had two slides and a Tarzan rope. Mr. Daniels had built it himself.

Chantelle skidded around the corner, almost

tripping over Chelsea, Jolene's little sister. She paused long enough to tag her.

"You're out!" she cried. "Go wait in the treehouse till I get Jolene."

Jolene had stopped just a few steps ahead. She waited until Chantelle was almost close enough to tag her, then grabbed the Tarzan rope and launched herself off the deck.

"Bye!" she called as she swooped through the air, her dark hair flapping behind her.

Chantelle didn't waste any time. She jumped onto the slide and shot down, hitting the ground just seconds after Jolene. Before Jolene could get away, Chantelle bounced to her feet and tagged her.

"Gotcha!" she cried. "Hah!" Both girls fell back into the snow, giggling and out of breath.

Treehouse Tag was one of their favorite games. Jolene, eight, could climb up and down the tree like a monkey. She wasn't afraid of anything. She was usually the last one to be caught.

"Pretty fun, eh?" Jolene said. "I almost got away. I was going to climb back up the other slide and sneak up behind you again."

"I thought you said we couldn't touch the ground!" Chantelle said. "You cheated."

"That was last time, remember? This time we just had to stay between the tree and the shed."

The sky was winter white, the trees in the Daniels' back yard all bare. It was late November in Chitek Lake, a tiny Canadian village in the Saskatchewan province. In Canada, a province is sort of like a state in America.

Chelsea slid down to join them. "I'm getting cold," she complained. "Let's go inside for a while."

Jolene shrugged. "OK. Chantelle and I can teach you some more jazz steps, eh?" Like many Canadians, Jolene often added "eh?" to the end of sentences to turn them into questions.

"Sure!" Chelsea said. "Let's go!"

The three of them raced to the door, peeling off layers of coats, sweaters, and boots as they stepped inside. The Daniels family lived in a cheerful brown house with lots of windows and a big downstairs playroom. The girls in the neighborhood loved the playroom. It had a large doll house, a play kitchen, a box of dress-up clothes and other things. Upstairs, there was also a big-screen TV and a piano. Mrs. Daniels was a nurse, but she also gave piano lessons on the side. She played the organ at church.

The girls had jazz music blasting when Mr. Daniels trotted down the steps. Grinning, he waited for them to notice him. Jolene finally looked up.

"Hi, Dad!" she yelled. "We're teaching Chelsea some dance steps!"

Mr. Daniels had a thick, dark mustache that stretched out when he smiled. "I see that!" he yelled back. "Turn down the music for a minute, eh? I wanted to ask you something!"

Chantelle clicked off the tape.

"Ah, that's better," Mr. Daniels said. "Hey, Jolene, how about taking your Honda out for a quick ride with me before it gets too dark?"

"OK!" Jolene exclaimed. "Is that all right with you, Chantelle? I won't be gone long. You can stay here if you want, and we can play some more after I get back."

Her friend smiled. "That's OK. It's almost supper time anyway, so I'd better go home."

Jolene bundled back up and followed her dad outside. She was still getting used to having him around the house again. His job putting asphalt on roads meant that he traveled a lot from May to November. It was always like a celebration when he came home to stay just weeks before Christmas.

A COLD RIDE

Jolene had a Honda trike, a motorcycle with three wheels. Her dad drove a bigger Honda. They liked to speed over the narrow trails that snaked through the "bush," the thick evergreen forests that dotted the area.

"Here's your helmet, JoJo," Mr. Daniels said, tossing it to her. "Make sure you put it on good and tight. Never can tell when you'll need it, eh?"

Jolene smiled. Two years before, when she had first gotten the trike, she had learned that lesson the hard way. After several days of "driving lessons," she had revved up the Honda and followed her dad out into the bush. She was sure she wouldn't have any problem.

Mr. Daniels had taken it slow at first. Jolene stayed close behind him, afraid to let him out of her sight. They started into the woods, leaving tire tracks in the snow.

Jolene was having a great time until her dad decided to speed up. Before she knew it, she was falling behind. She was afraid to go much faster. It already felt like she was going fifty miles per hour! When her father roared out of sight around a bend in the trail ahead, she panicked.

"Dad, wait!" she yelled. "Let me catch up!" But the bush muffled her voice. He couldn't hear her.

Jolene sped up, not realizing how sharp the next turn was. Halfway around it, her trike skidded sideways, then flipped. Jolene flew off over the handlebars and landed hard in the snow. The trike ran over her.

Luckily, all it did was bruise her legs. By the time her dad doubled back to find her, she was sitting up, crying and brushing snow out of her hair. She had walked back home that day. Ever since, she had been careful to take corners nice and slow.

Today, though, their ride went smoothly. By the time they got back home, supper was ready.

"Your cheeks are red!" Mrs. Daniels exclaimed when they walked in, both wearing big smiles. "You'd better come and warm up!"

"We're all right," Mr. Daniels said. "We're tough. Right, JoJo?"

"Right." Jolene sniffed the air. "Mmm, it smells good in here. What's for dinner, Mum? I'm starving."

"Lasagna."

"Good! I'll go get Chelsea." Jolene dashed out, her dark curls bouncing. Even after playing hard all afternoon, she still had a lot of energy left over. She liked to stay busy.

Over supper, Mrs. Daniels announced that she had volunteered to work at school the next morning. Chitek Lake was too small to have its own school, so Jolene and Chelsea both went to school in Leoville. Grades kindergarden through twelfth all went to Leoville Central School.

"You can ride with me tomorrow instead of taking the bus," Mrs. Daniels said. "That way you won't have to wake up so early."

"Good!" Jolene said. "I hate riding the bus."

The next morning, when they were ready to leave for school, Jolene bounced into the kitchen. "Mum, if you'll give me the keys to the van, I'll go start it and let it warm up."

Mrs. Daniels smiled. Ever since the day her husband had shown Jolene how to start the family minivan, she had decided it was her job.

"OK," Mrs. Daniels said, digging in her purse for the keys. "Just don't touch the gear shift, eh?"

"I won't."

On the way to Leoville, they talked about their Christmas plans.

"This weekend I'm going to make some caramel turtles, and probably some sugar cookies, too," Mrs. Daniels said. "You girls can help if you want."

"I'll decorate the sugar cookies," Chelsea offered. "I like doing that."

"And I'll help make the turtles," Jolene said. "They're my favorites. Are we going to make some for Grandma Benny, too?"

Mrs. Daniels nodded. "Sure. We can take her and Grandma Rita a big box at Christmas. That is, if we can keep your dad from eating them all before then!"

"Doris Daniels!" Jolene said in her most grownup tone. "How can you say something like that about our very own father?"

"Watch it, you," Mrs. Daniels said. "I'm still 'Mum' to you. And your very own father sneaks cookies and turtles every time I turn my back. He's even worse than you two." Jolene and Chelsea giggled.

The next week passed in a happy blur of Christmas shopping, baking, and decorating. Jolene and Chelsea strung tinsel garlands around the house, sprayed fake "snow" on the windows, and hung their Christmas stockings. Both girls practiced for their parts in Christmas plays at school. Mrs. Daniels practiced playing the piano for the town Christmas concert. Mr. Daniels practiced sneaking Christmas cookies.

"It puts me in the holiday spirit," he joked each time he got caught.

Two weeks before Christmas, they all agreed it was time to get a tree. They never bought Christmas trees; they just went out into the bush and cut them fresh.

"Who wants to help me pick out the tree this year?" Mr. Daniels asked. "Chelsea?"

Chelsea was busy playing with some friends. "I don't want to this time," she said. "I'd rather stay here."

CHRISTMAS TREE SEARCH

Jolene rolled her eyes. "I'll go, Dad."

Bouncing along in her dad's pickup truck a few minutes later, Jolene watched out the window for deer. Small herds could sometimes be seen grazing right beside the road. She liked to watch them.

"Look!" Mr. Daniels exclaimed. Off to the left, a doe had raised her head to watch them pass. Her tail was twitching nervously, but she didn't run. Mr. Daniels smiled. "Looks like she made it through the hunting season this year, eh?"

Hunting season had just ended the week before. In November and early December, Americans often came to Canada to hunt deer. Sometimes they paid Mr. Daniels to guide them and set up tree stands where they could sit high in trees, watching for the deer. Mr. Daniels didn't hunt, but he liked to video-tape the deer and other wildlife out in the bush.

Jolene sighed and leaned back against the tall seat. "Dad, can I steer for a minute? There's nobody else around."

Mr. Daniels shrugged. "I guess so. Come sit on my knee so you can see."

Jolene scooted over and grabbed the steering wheel. Even on her father's knee, she could barely see over the dashboard. Mr. Daniels kept his hands on the wheel, just in case. They were going slow, but he didn't want Jolene accidentally to run them into a ditch. "You can't just hold the wheel straight," he said. "You have to move it sometimes to keep the truck going in a straight line."

Jolene nodded. "Like this?" She turned the wheel a little to the right. They were going so slow it took a minute for the truck to straighten out.

"I guess so. You've got it, eh?"

Jolene said proudly, "I bet I'll be a good driver when I'm older. I already know how to drive my three-wheeler, and now I know how to drive your truck."

"Whoa, not quite," Mr. Daniels said. "All you're doing is *steering*. There's a lot more to driving than that."

Jolene made a face. "I know that, Dad," she said. "You have to use the gas and brake pedals, too."

"Good for you. But that still doesn't mean you know how to drive." They were coming up on a curve. "Here, let me steer around this turn."

"Let me try," Jolene pleaded. "I can do it!"

Mr. Daniels sighed. "OK, OK. But take it easy. Remember your crash on the Honda? You aren't exactly great on turns."

"That was when I was six, Dad. I haven't wrecked in a long time."

"Now there's a comforting thought." As they came up to the curve, Mr. Daniels slowed down. Jolene frowned. She wanted to impress her dad by doing this just right. Gripping the steering wheel tightly, she turned it a little to the left.

Nothing happened.

"Turn it a little farther," Mr. Daniels said. "You have to keep turning it until the truck goes where you want it to."

Jolene turned the wheel a little more. The truck slowly started around the curve. She relaxed. "See?" she said coolly. "I told you I could do it."

Mr. Daniels chuckled. "Not bad for a woman driver. Especially one who's too short to reach the pedals!" He lifted her off his knee. "Go ahead and scoot back over now. We need to go find our Christmas tree."

When they spotted some small spruce trees, Mr. Daniels pulled off the road. He and Jolene tramped through the snow to look at them.

Jolene examined them all before pointing to her favorite. "Let's cut that one, Dad. It's cute . . . kind of short and fat."

"Cute?" Mr. Daniels said, making fun of her. "You want a *cute* Christmas tree?"

"Yes. You said I could pick. I want the cute one."

Mr. Daniels reached into the back of the truck to pull out his axe. "OK. But you have to stand here by the truck while I cut down your cute little tree. I wouldn't want to accidentally cut down my cute little daughter."

"Your cute *little* daughter is at home," Jolene shot back. "I'm your cute *big* daughter."

"My mistake. I forgot you're driving now. What's next, eh? You planning to get married anytime soon?"

Jolene giggled. "Not till I turn nine."

"That's good. I don't approve of these young marriages. Women should be at least ten or eleven before they get married."

Mr. Daniels quickly cut down the tree, then

threw it into the back of the truck. He and Jolene laughed most of the way home.

Mrs. Daniels saw them when they pulled into the drive. She held the door open so they could carry in the tree. Mr. Daniels paused on the doorstep to shake the snow off its branches.

"What a nice tree!" Mrs. Daniels said. "You can take it right into the living room. I already set up the stand."

"I picked it out," Jolene told her.

"Well, it looks nice and full. You did a good job."

They waited until after supper to decorate the tree. Jolene and Chelsea hung their favorite ornaments, then draped silver tinsel over the branches. When they were finished, Mrs. Daniels plugged in the lights. The tree didn't look cute anymore; it looked beautiful.

"I love Christmas," Jolene sighed. "It's my favorite time of year. Especially since Dad gets to be home."

Mr. Daniels leaned over to tweak one of her curls. "I like Christmas, too." He grinned. "Especially since I get to steal all the cookies you girls bake."

"Dad!" Jolene and Chelsea said together.

The last two weeks before Christmas always seemed to last two months. Jolene could hardly wait to see what she was getting this year. She had hinted and hinted that she wanted a Karaoke machine. She hoped her parents had been listening.

Finally, though, it was Christmas Eve. That

morning, Mrs. Daniels went to choir practice and Chelsea went to play at Grandma Rita's. Jolene and Mr. Daniels were the only ones left at home.

"Well, JoJo," Mr. Daniels said, "I've got an idea. Let's drive out to Grandma and Grandpa Larrivee's farm, eh? We can take them their presents and cookies and visit for a while. And maybe on the way home, we can stop and put up that new tree stand. I picked out the perfect spot for it."

Grandma and Grandpa Larrivee were really Mr. Daniels' foster parents. He had been only seven when he and his baby brother had gone into foster care. The Larrivees, a loving elderly couple who had raised five kids of their own, had eventually taken in both boys. Jolene loved visiting their small farm.

"Want me to get the cookies and stuff for Grandma Benny?" she asked. Mrs. Larrivee's first name was Benny, and Jolene had always called her "Grandma Benny."

"Sure. You can do that while I hook up the Ski-Doo trailer to my truck." The Ski-Doo was a snowmobile. "We'll have to cross a couple of fields to get to the tree where I want to put the stand. We'll have to park the truck and Ski-Doo the rest of the way."

A few minutes later, they were on their way. Jolene insisted on holding the colorful box of Christmas cookies on her lap.

"I'm going to make sure you don't eat them on the way," she said. "I don't want to show up at Grandma and Grandpa's with just a plate of crumbs."

"Would I do that?" Mr. Daniels joked.

"Yes."

"You're probably right."

The Larrivee's farm was about twenty-five miles away, out in the country. To get there, they had to turn off the paved highway onto a gravel road, then drive another three or four miles through rolling hills. In the summer it was a short drive. But now, with four or five inches of snow on the roads, they had to take it slow.

TO GRANDMA'S HOUSE WE GO

Jolene watched out the window as they weaved along. When she saw a field with rows of round hay bales lined up in the snow, she knew they were getting close. Her grandparents had lots of land and cattle.

Finally, they rounded the last big curve. The farmhouse popped into view, perched at the top of a hill. The Larrivee's house was small but painted a cheerful blue. Next to it was a pond, frozen solid this time of year.

Mr. Daniels pulled into the yard. "Let's sneak in and surprise them," he said. "I didn't tell them we were coming."

Jolene grinned. A moment later she followed him up the steps and into the house, trying not to make too much noise. As soon as they walked in, though, Grandma Benny came bustling around the corner.

"Hi, Grandma!" Jolene cried, running over to

hug her. "We brought you some Christmas cookies!"

Her grandmother leaned down to kiss her. "Ah, Grandma's girl!" she said, beaming. "Thank you so much!"

Mr. Daniels kissed her on the cheek. "Merry Christmas, Mum!"

Grandma Benny was so short that she had to tilt her face up to look at him. "Merry Christmas, my boy! But you didn't have to bring presents. Come say hello to your dad and the boys." Mr. Daniels' three foster brothers were down for Christmas. After greeting them, Mr. Daniels and Jolene sat down to one of Grandma Benny's big, country-style lunches.

"So, Jolene, where's your sister?" Uncle Louis asked. "And your mum?"

"Mum's at choir practice, and Chelsea's at my other grandma's. She wanted to go play with all our cousins that are visiting. They're all girls, you know."

"Really?" said Uncle Robert. "Not a single boy cousin, eh?"

"Nope. Grandma Rita had three girls, then all *her* girls had girls. Lots of girls. I have eight girl cousins."

Uncle Louis pretended to shudder. "Sounds awful. No wonder you came here instead!"

Jolene laughed. "I'm going there tomorrow for Christmas dinner. I just like going around with my dad. We're stopping on the way home to put up his tree stand."

Uncle Louis looked at Mr. Daniels. "Where are you setting it up, Dale?"

"Oh, out in that far corner where the heavy spruce are," Mr. Daniels replied. "You know, over by Uncle Pete's old farm. There's a deer trail out there that follows a ravine."

"Oh, yes, I know the place. But with deer season over, why are you putting a stand up?"

"I'm planning to put my video camera up there sometime next month to film the deer. The weather's good today, and I thought while I was already out here, I'd get it out of the way."

It was around one o'clock when Jolene and her dad wished everybody a Merry Christmas and started back out to the truck. Grandma Benny stood at the door and waved as they pulled away.

"That was nice, eh?" Mr. Daniels said.

"Yes," Jolene sighed. "But I'm all stuffed now. I don't think I'll be hungry at supper time."

"Oh, well. Maybe we'll work up an appetite while we're out in the bush."

Jolene yawned. She felt like falling asleep as her father wound his way back down through the hills. The road was lined with snow-filled ditches, and in one spot it snaked along the edge of a fifty-foot drop. Jolene was glad she wasn't steering.

When they got to Uncle Pete's old farm, Mr. Daniels backed the truck around into the yard. He turned off the engine, but left the keys in the ignition. This far out in the country, they didn't have to worry about somebody stealing the truck.

"OK, let's get moving," he said. "I just want to

zip out there, put the stand up, then zip right back. We've got other things to do this afternoon."

Jolene helped him slide the Ski-Doo down off the trailer. Mr. Daniels loaded the tree stand onto the Ski-Doo, then pulled the starter cord. When the engine started, he swung his leg over the seat. Jolene scrambled up behind him and wrapped her arms around his waist.

"Ready?" he said. Jolene nodded. They took off across the field in a spray of snow.

Jolene held on tight. When she peeked out around her dad, the cold air hit her face. It was five degrees below zero outside. [Celsius, not Fahrenheit]. Her ski suit and heavy winter boots kept her body warm, but the wind made her eyes sting.

They zoomed along, leaving a wide track in the snow behind them. When they reached a locked gate, Mr. Daniels turned and drove along the fence until they came to an opening.

They had to drive over a mile before they reached the woods. Mr. Daniels guided the snowmobile through the trees and stopped near a ravine.

"That's the tree!" he said, pointing to a tall spruce growing at the bottom of the ravine. "I picked it out the last time I was here. Now I'll just climb up and hook on the stand. It won't take but a minute."

Jolene looked at the tree doubtfully. It was a lot taller than she had imagined. "You're going to climb up all that way?"

"Sure," Mr. Daniels said. "I do it all the time. It's no problem."

The branches did look nice and thick, Jolene told herself. And her dad had done this lots of times before. There was nothing to worry about.

Mr. Daniels hooked the tree stand over his shoulder. "We'll have to walk down the rest of the way. It's too steep for the Ski-Doo."

Jolene plodded down the slope beside him, her boots sinking into the snow. Partway down, he stopped and pointed to a spot off to one side.

"I want you to wait up here, out of the way," he said. "That way if I drop the tree stand, I won't drop it on you!"

Jolene didn't like the sound of that. "Be careful, OK, Dad?"

"Don't worry, I will. I always check the branches to make sure they can hold my weight before I step on them."

"Good." Jolene sank down and hugged her knees to her chest. She studied the spruce tree. It didn't look too hard to climb, she decided. It was tall, but the branches were solid.

Mr. Daniels reached the tree and pulled himself up on the lowest branch. Jolene watched as he climbed the first few feet. Then he paused.

"Jolene!" he called.

Jolene stood up. "What, Dad?"

"Listen. Just in case I happen to fall, you might have to go get help, eh? We're kind of out in the middle of nowhere. If I got knocked unconscious or something, I wouldn't be able to talk to you."

His words scared her. "Dad . . ." she began.

"Hey, look, nothing like that is going to happen," Mr. Daniels said quickly. "But just in case, I wanted you to know what to do. Nobody's expecting us at home, and Grandma and Grandpa don't expect us to come back. Nobody would know to come look for us for a long time. You'd have to go get help."

Jolene didn't say anything else. But as her father started back up again, her heart was pounding. Why did he have to say something like that? Now she was all nervous.

She kept her eyes on him every second, as if she could make him stick to the tree that way. He climbed higher and higher, using his hands and feet like a tree spider. By the time he was thirty-five feet up, Jolene had to lean back to see him.

She was just starting to relax when it happened. Her dad had reached the spot where he wanted to hook on the stand. He stopped, hanging onto a branch with one hand while he used the other to slide the tree stand down off his shoulder. Suddenly, the branch under his feet snapped with a sharp *crack*!

TERROR IN THE BUSH

Mr. Daniels' startled yelp sent Jolene leaping to her feet. She watched as he grabbed for the tree trunk, but the stand got in his way. He slammed against the tree and then bounced backward. His boots thrashed in the air as he tried to wrap his legs around another branch.

Then the branch above him broke off in his hand. With a terrified yell, Mr. Daniels came crashing down, feet-first, through the branches.

"Dad!" Jolene screamed in horror. "No!"

The next few seconds seemed to pass in slow-motion for the terrified eight-year-old. Still screaming, she ran down the slope, fighting her way through the deep snow. Her dad's body hit branch after branch, snapping them off on the way down. She could hear his screams even over her own.

He's going to die, Jolene thought. *Dad's going to die. There'll be no more Dad now.*

She was still a few feet away when he hit the ground. His feet hit first, then his whole body just seemed to crumple. He pitched forward into the snow like a broken rag doll.

Jolene stopped short. *"No!"* she cried. Her sobbing wail seemed to echo through the lonely woods.

Moving like she was in a nightmare, Jolene stumbled forward and knelt beside him. "Dad!" she moaned. "Dad!"

Mr. Daniels didn't answer. Then, slowly, he opened his eyes. His nose was bleeding, and his face was grey with pain. Jolene leaned close, afraid to touch him. "Dad, are you OK?" she sobbed.

"Jolene?" he murmured.

Jolene could hardly talk. "I'm right here." She could see that her dad's legs were twisted around under him. She knew without being told that he was in trouble.

"I need help," Mr. Daniels whispered. "I'm hurting really bad."

"What can I do?" She didn't know any first aid. She was only in the third grade.

"I need you to put my legs back the way they're supposed to look. Then I want you to turn me over onto my side."

Jolene was horrified. "But I'll hurt you!" she cried.

"It doesn't matter. I'm already hurting. But if I black out and start throwing up, I'll choke to death unless I'm turned on my side. OK?"

"OK. I'll try."

Following her father's instructions, she gently straightened his legs one at a time. Mr. Daniels groaned a few times, but he told her to keep going. By the time she finished, her hands were shaking. Mr. Daniels nodded, trying to hide his pain. "That's good. Now see if you can roll me up on my side."

Biting her lip, Jolene did as he asked. She tried not to look at his face. She knew she was hurting him. When she was done, he looked up at her.

"Thanks. That's much better. Now I need you to go get help. Go back to the farm and get Grandpa and Uncle Louis. They'll know where I am."

Jolene stared at him. "Dad, I can't leave you here! You've got to come with me!"

Mr. Daniels clenched his teeth and tried to move. The effort made him gasp in pain.

"I can't do it, JoJo," he said. "I can't even feel my legs. I need you to get help. If you don't . . ." He let his words trail away.

Jolene looked around at the empty woods. They

were miles from anywhere. "How do I get back to the farm?"

"You'll have to ride the Ski-Doo. Just follow the tracks back to the road. From there you'll know where to go."

Jolene nodded, her eyes blurred with tears. "OK, Dad. I'll do it."

Jumping up, she ran back up the slope to the snowmobile. She had never started it before, but she had watched her dad do it lots of times. She grabbed the pull-cord, braced her feet and yanked it as hard as she could.

Nothing happened.

She tried again, this time using both hands. Still nothing. The engine didn't even try to start. Frustrated, she yanked the cord again and again. It had to start, it just *had* to!

Nothing.

She finally gave up and ran back down to her father. "I can't start it," she said tearfully. "I'm not strong enough."

She wasn't even sure at first that he had heard her. His eyes were closed, and he was breathing hard. But then he sighed.

"You'll have to walk," he said. "If you can get back to the truck, you can drive it to the farm."

Jolene couldn't believe what she was hearing. "I can't drive your truck! Not by myself!"

Mr. Daniels drew a shaky breath. "You can do it, Jo. You'll just have to go very slow, and steer like I showed you." He added, "You'll have to be very brave for me."

Jolene felt like her heart was going to explode with sadness. "OK, Dad, I'll try. Just tell me what to do. I know how to start it, but I don't know how to make it drive. I've never done that before."

Mr. Daniels rested for a minute before speaking again. "OK," he said. "It's really easy. You know the gear shift that sticks out by the steering wheel?"

"I think so."

"Once you start the truck, you just pull that stick straight down. The little arrow that tells you what gear you're in is broken off, so you can't go by that. You'll just have to make sure you pull it *all the way down*. Understand?"

"What will that do?"

"It will put the truck in low gear. That should help keep you from going too fast. After you put it in gear, you just push the gas pedal and start driving."

He looked up at her. "You'll have to go slow. The Ski-Doo trailer is hooked onto the back. I don't think you can unhook it by yourself. It's going to make the truck a lot harder to steer. You'll have to take it slow or you'll go off into a ditch."

Jolene nodded, seeing the worry in his face. "I'll be careful, Dad. Don't worry."

With one last look at her father's crumpled body, she started back up the slope. It wasn't going to be easy. She would have to walk over a mile through deep snow, then drive a heavy pickup truck another three miles. But her dad was counting on her. She couldn't let him down.

BRAVERY IN THE FACE OF FEAR

The wind took Jolene's breath away as she stepped out of the trees. She had no trouble finding the snowmobile tracks, but it took all of her energy to run through the snow. She had barely taken twenty steps, and she was already exhausted.

I've got to keep going, she thought. *I've got to get help for Dad before he freezes*. The thought made her run even faster.

After a while she lost track of time. Despite the terrible cold, she was sweating. She pulled off her gloves, then her knit headband. *Keep running*, she told herself. *Don't stop*. Tears were frozen on her cheeks, but she was so cold and scared that she didn't notice.

It seemed like hours before she reached the locked gate. The Ski-Doo tracks led off to her left, where she and her dad had driven around it earlier. But Jolene quickly decided it would waste too much time to go that way. She climbed over the fence and dropped down on the other side. It only took her a few minutes to find the Ski-Doo tracks again.

Finally, the weary eight-year-old looked up to see her father's truck. With a cry of relief, she ran up and climbed inside. At least she had made it this far!

She tossed her gloves and headband onto the seat beside her and reached for the key. The truck *had* to start, she told herself. If it didn't, she would have to run the whole three miles to her grandparents' farm. She didn't think she could make it.

"Please let it start," she prayed aloud as she turned the key. "Please!"

The engine started the first time. Jolene sighed with relief. But now she faced another big problem. How was she going to drive? Her legs were too short to reach the pedals. And even if she could reach the pedals sitting down, she wouldn't be able to see over the dashboard!

I'll just have to drive standing up, she decided. *It's the only way.*

Jolene held herself up by the steering wheel and felt for the gas pedal with her foot. By stretching, she could just touch it with her toes. It would work.

She took a deep breath. It was now or never.

Keeping a firm grip on the steering wheel, Jolene stepped on the gas pedal. The engine roared louder, but the truck didn't move. Why wouldn't it go?

Then she remembered what her father had said about the gear shift stick. Still stepping on the gas pedal, she yanked the stick all the way down in one quick movement.

What happened next took her by surprise. The heavy truck leaped forward with a jerk, flinging her backward. She gasped as it bounced and jolted over the snowy ground. It was going too fast!

Sobbing with fear, Jolene jerked the steering wheel. The truck swerved right and skidded onto the driveway. Heart pounding, Jolene peeked over the dashboard to see that she was heading straight for the gravel road. If she could turn right again at the road, she would be heading back toward the farm.

The tires slipped and skidded, but the truck made the turn. Blinking back tears, Jolene stepped on the gas again. She had to get to Grandma Benny's fast!

She did all right for the first few hundred yards. But then she let the truck's right tires drift off the edge of the road. The next thing she knew, she was bumping over the snow again.

Shrieking, she turned the wheel in the other direction. The pickup swerved sharply. Now it was heading for a ditch on the other side of the road!

"I can't do this!" Jolene gasped. "I don't know how to drive!" Each time she jerked the wheel, the truck zig-zagged. The Ski-Doo trailer was also weaving back and forth, making it even worse.

Terrified, Jolene thought of her mother, miles away at choir practice. If only she knew what was happening. If only she had come along! The thought suddenly made her feel weak. She needed help!

"Please, God," Jolene cried aloud. "Please help me and my dad!"

After several more tries, she got the truck to stop zig-zagging. Jolene stared straight ahead, trying not to cry. *I can't crash*, she told herself. *If I do, Dad will freeze.*

Driving wasn't as easy as she had always thought. The road was slippery and covered with snow. At every curve, she was afraid she would slide off into a ditch. What scared her most, though, was the thought of the steep hills just ahead. If she skidded off the edge there, nobody would find her—or her dad—until too late.

"Please help me," she whispered. "Help me do this!"

Jolene made it safely around several more twists and turns in the road. When she came to the fifty-foot drop she and her dad had passed earlier, though, she couldn't help being scared. The road there was very narrow, with the slope on one side and a ditch on the other.

I'll have to steer right down the middle of the road, Jolene told herself. If the truck started zigzagging again, she would be in trouble. But she had no other choice. Pointing the truck straight ahead, Jolene pressed on the gas.

She was almost too scared to breathe as the heavy pickup bumped forward over the snow and gravel. She tried not to look as she got closer to the slope. Her hands on the steering wheel were sweating.

Then she felt the trailer start to weave.

"Oh, no!" she moaned. If the trailer slid off, wouldn't it pull the whole truck down? In a panic, she turned away from the edge. She would rather drive into a ditch than off a cliff!

Jolene was tossed back and forth as the front tires ran off the pavement. Screaming, she frantically turned the wheel in the other direction. The truck bounced back onto the gravel. She had made it past the cliff!

Jolene took several deep breaths to steady herself. *I'm almost there*, she told herself. *I won't have to do this much longer*. The thought that the ordeal was almost over calmed her.

Less than five minutes later, she drove around the curve to see her grandparents' farmhouse. Somehow, the sight of the cheerful blue house with Christmas lights blinking made all her courage disappear. She burst into tears. By the time she got to the top of the drive, she could hardly see.

She rolled to a stop, turned off the truck, and threw open the door.

"Grandma!" she sobbed, jumping down from the truck. She was trying to shout, but she was crying too hard. "Uncle Louis!"

The minute Jolene jumped out, however, the truck started rolling backwards down the hill. She gasped and ran to stop it. Luckily, she had left the driver's door open. Jumping back inside, she stepped on the brake, then shoved the gear shift stick all the way back up, just like her dad had left it.

A moment later she burst in through the Larravee's front door. Hearing voices in the living room, she ran around the corner.

Her grandparents and all three of her uncles were sitting there, talking and laughing. They looked up, surprised, when she ran in crying.

"Help!" she sobbed. "My dad fell out of a tree!"

Uncle Louis jumped up from the couch. He didn't ask any questions. "I'll call an ambulance!" he said.

Grandma Larravee's face was pale as she

rushed over to Jolene. "Oh, my dear," she said, hugging her. "It's all right. It's going to be all right."

Jolene couldn't catch her breath. "But Dad can't feel his legs! He says they're both broken!"

Uncle Louis came back into the living room. "The ambulance is on its way. I told them where to go, but they won't be able to get there in the ambulance. We'll have to take the tractor out and clear a path for them."

"Do you want me to go along and show them where he is?" Jolene asked. "I can take them right to him."

Grandpa Larravee patted her shoulder. "No, you just stay here with your grandma. The boys and I will make sure they find him, don't you worry."

Grandpa Larravee, Uncle Louis, Uncle Omer, and Uncle Robert all threw on coats and rushed out the door. Grandma Benny led Jolene over to the couch.

Jolene sat down and covered her face. "I'm scared, Grandma," she sobbed. Now that she had time to think about everything, she couldn't stop shivering. "I don't want Dad to die."

Grandma Benny was also crying. "Of course you don't, dear," she said. "I'm going to call your mother and then we'll sit right here and pray for your dad. All right?"

"OK."

Mrs. Daniels was still at choir practice. Since there was no phone at the church, Grandma

Benny sent somebody to tell her what had happened.

"Your mum is going to come straight here," she told Jolene when she came back. "Then she'll take you to the hospital so you can wait for your dad."

"I was afraid he was going to freeze," Jolene said tearfully. "I drove here as fast as I could. I almost went into a bunch of ditches."

"You did just fine."

Jolene huddled on the couch and listened as the elderly woman prayed. She was still too scared and upset to pray, but she agreed with every word Grandma Benny said.

Finally, Mrs. Daniels pulled up in the van. Jolene ran outside.

"Dad fell out of a tree!" she said and started crying again. "I had to drive his truck all the way here!"

Mrs. Daniels hugged her. "I know, JoJo, I know. I found out they're supposed to take your father to Spiritwood Hospital. Let's go there and wait for him."

A GRATEFUL FATHER

At the hospital, Jolene couldn't settle down. Had they found him yet? If so, what was taking them so long? It had already been almost two hours. Several ambulances screamed up, but her father wasn't in any of them.

Where *was* he?

I should have gone with Grandpa and Uncle Louis, Jolene thought miserably. *I should have shown them right where he was.* What if he was still lying out there all alone? He would think she had just given up!

Just then, another ambulance arrived. Jolene and Mrs. Daniels jumped up and raced outside. When the ambulance doors opened, Jolene saw her father's dark hair and mustache.

"It's Dad!" she said.

She watched anxiously as the emergency medical technicians (EMTs) lifted him out. He was bundled up in lots of blankets, but his eyes were open. The EMTs quickly carried him into the emergency room. Jolene and her mom followed them in, then trotted along beside them.

Mrs. Daniels spoke first. "How are you feeling?"

Mr. Daniels looked up at her, his face pale. "I'll be OK," he said. "I'm just so cold."

Jolene wanted to talk to him. She wanted to tell him that she had gotten help for him as fast as she could. But the minute she opened her mouth, she burst into tears again. Before she could stop crying, the EMTs had whisked her father away into a small room.

Mrs. Daniels went inside with him, but Jolene stayed in the hall. She remembered how it had hurt him when she tried to straighten his legs out in the woods. She couldn't bear to watch him get hurt again. After the doctors looked at Mr. Daniels, though, Mrs. Daniels walked back out and waved to Jolene.

"Can you come in here?" she said. "They've decided to move your dad to the hospital in Saskatoon, but he wants to talk to you first."

Jolene nodded. Inside, she walked over to her father's bedside. "Hi, Dad," she said.

"Come here, my girl. How are you doing?"

"I'm OK. Are you . . . ?"

Mr. Daniels smiled weakly. "Well, it looks like I broke my legs and maybe some other stuff. But once the doctors fix me up, I should be fine."

He reached out and took her hand. "I just wanted you to know that I'm really proud of you. There aren't many kids your age who could've done what you did. I knew I could count on you."

"Really?"

"Really."

For the first time since she'd heard the branch snap under her father's foot, Jolene relaxed. She squeezed his hand. "I was afraid you were going to freeze. And then, when you didn't show up for so long, I was afraid they hadn't found you. I was afraid you might be thinking I gave up or something."

"Never crossed my mind. Anyway, they came for me pretty fast. It just took a while for them to pull me up out of the ravine. They had to use a sled."

At the Saskatoon hospital, the doctors found out that Mr. Daniels' legs *and* hips were broken. There was no way he could have gotten help without Jolene. He went into surgery, then was put in the Intensive Care Unit.

The next morning, on Christmas Day, Jolene and Chelsea got up early and gathered up all their dad's presents. They had opened all of theirs late the night before. Mrs. Daniels had promised to drive them to Saskatoon that morning.

At the hospital, Jolene sat close to her father, helping him open his gifts. He was still pretty weak, and he couldn't talk since he had a tube in his throat. He had to write little notes on a pad.

He looked bad, but Jolene still marveled that he was there at all. It was hard to believe that just yesterday, he had been lying out in the snow near death.

After the last package was opened, Mr. Daniels smiled weakly and wrote: "Thanks."

"Now we'll just have to get you out of here so you can use some of this stuff," Mrs. Daniels said. "I wish you could have been there last night to see the girls open their gifts. Jolene finally got the karaoke machine she's been hinting about for months!" She looked over at Jolene. "I guess that was your favorite gift this year, eh?"

Jolene thought, then shook her head. "I liked the karaoke machine a lot," she said, "but it wasn't my *favorite*." She smiled at her father, then took his hand. "Yesterday, I was thinking that I wasn't going to have a dad anymore. So I think my favorite present this year is getting Dad back."

Jolene Daniels, eight-year-old hero, was awarded the Medal of Bravery. She also received an award for heroism from the Canadian Red Cross.

Kids! Have you heard or read about someone who should be a "Real Kid"? We're always looking for new stories for future volumes of *Real Kids, Real Adventures*—true stories about young survivors and heroes. If you've heard about a story that might work, send a newspaper clipping or other information to:

REAL KIDS, REAL ADVENTURES
STORY TIPS
P.O. BOX 461572
GARLAND, TEXAS 75046-1572

You can also E-mail us at: *storytips@realkids.com*. Remember to include your name and phone number in case we need to contact you.

If your story is chosen for use in a future volume of *Real Kids, Real Adventures* (and you were the first one to send that particular story in), you will receive a free, autographed copy of the book and have your name mentioned at the end of the story.

Visit the Real Kids Real Adventures™ Web site at:

http://www.realkids.com

Win a free

EUROPEAN ADVENTURE

or a DYNO VFR BIKE!

If you're a "real kid" who loves adventure, this is the contest for you! To enter, just write a story or essay on the subject: "My Greatest Adventure." Winners will be chosen from two age categories: 8–12, and 13–17.

The winner in the 13–17 age category will join other adventurous teens and professional guides for an exciting 21-day summer European adventure, sponsored by Venture Europe. If you win, you'll go white-water rafting and canyoning in France...mountain biking in Italy...backpacking across vast Alpine glaciers and peaks in Switzerland. It'll be three weeks of nonstop adventure!

The winner in the 8–12 age group will win a brand-new Dyno VFR bicycle, complete with a *Real Kids, Real Adventures* helmet, knee pads, and backpack survival kit. If you win, you'll be prepared for adventure wherever you go!

....

CONTEST RULES:

1. Your story or essay must be 1,000 words or less (or a maximum of four, double-spaced typewritten pages). It can be either fiction or nonfiction. Your entry must include your name, age, birthdate, mailing address, phone number, and the name of your parent(s) or legal guardian. Only *one* entry allowed per person.

2. **The deadline for all entries is April 30th, 1998.** Entries postmarked after April 30th will not be considered, and no entries will be returned. Entries should be mailed to: *Real Kids, Real Adventures Contest*, P.O. Box 461572, Garland, Texas 75046-1572.

3. The winner in the 13–17 age category will receive a free "Ultimate Alps" adventure trip from America's Adventure/Venture Europe. Round-trip airfare to Geneva, Switzerland, to meet the Venture Europe team will be provided from the nearest international airport in the U.S. or Canada.

4. Travel costs for transporting the winner to and from an international airport will be the responsibility of the winner's family. Some physical/legal restrictions apply relating to a winner's participation in the Ultimate Alps adventure. All prizes are nontransferrable. All prizes must be redeemed by **August 1999**.

5. The winner in the 8–12 age category will receive a free Dyno VFR bicycle, complete with a *Real Kids, Real Adventures* helmet, knee pads, and backpack survival kit.

6. This contest is open to all U.S. and Canadian residents ages 8–17. Void where prohibited by law. Sponsored by America's Adventure. The Berkley Publishing Group and its affiliates, successors and assigns are not responsible for any claims or injuries of contestants in connection with the contest or prizes.

America's Adventure, Inc.
2245 Stonecrop Way
Golden, CO 80401-8524, USA
Email: adventur76@aol.com
http://www.realkids.com/AA-VE

Venture Europe
Kerkstraat 34, B9830
Sint-Martens Latem, Belgium, Europe
Email: roelver@pophost.eunet.be